PAPER GHOSTS

A NOVEL BY

MIKE RESTAINO

To Erin —

Enjoy!

[signature]

PAPER GHOSTS

Mike Restaino

www.paperghostsbook.com

ISBN 978-1-54391-512-9

Library of Congress Control Number: 2017958323

Some characters and events in this book are fictitious. Any similarity to real persons, living or dead, is coincidental and not intended by the author.

Cover art and design by Mike Miller
RISE Designs – South Lake Tahoe, CA
www.risegraphics.com

Author photo by Marc Roberts

Printed and Bound in The United States of America

First Printing: 2018

To Rebecca and Ryan

Everything is wonderful, and microscopes are fun!
- ROBERT POLLARD

1

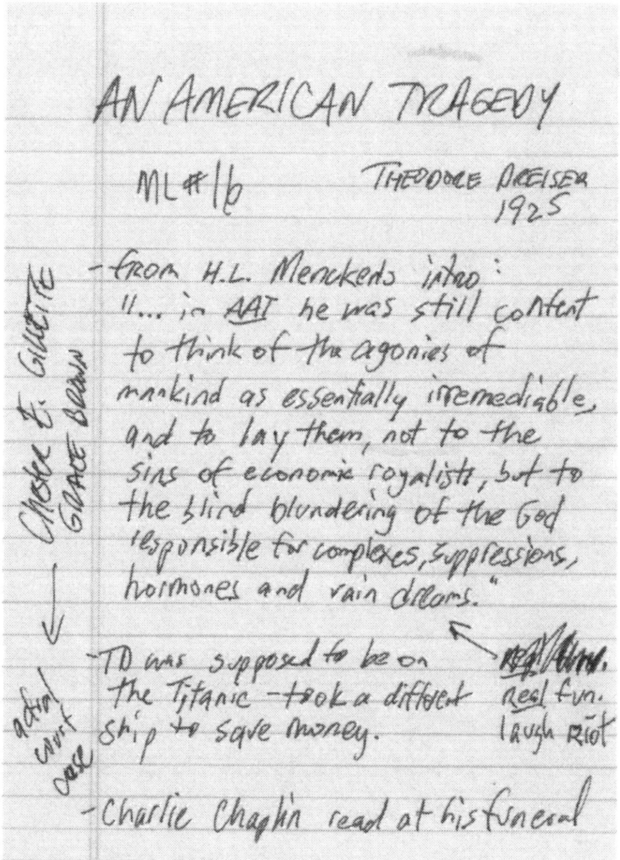

AN AMERICAN TRAGEDY

ML#16

THEODORE DREISER
1925

Chester E. Gillette
Grace Brown
← actual court case

- from H.L. Mencken's intro:
"... in AAT he was still content to think of the agonies of mankind as essentially irremediable, and to lay them, not to the sins of economic royalists, but to the blind blundering of the God responsible for complexes, suppressions, hormones and vain dreams."

[illegible] real fun. laugh riot

- TD was supposed to be on the Titanic - took a different ship to save money.

- Charlie Chaplin read at his funeral

2

"That is the stupidest idea I've ever heard."

Dalton Ross sipped his seven-dollar coffee after the words left his mouth. Across the table, Luke Sullivan felt a sudden sting of paranoia, convinced that a nameless passer-by on the swirling New York City sidewalk behind them had overheard his folly, recognized him, and hurriedly crossed Broadway while quietly damning the idiocy displayed by *the guy from that one TV show.*

On any other Thursday, Luke would have ignored a delusional hiccup like this with the warm assistance of a cup of coffee or six, but he had opted to abstain from caffeine's jittery lurch during his nerve-wracking midday summit. Idly spinning an ice water and dreading further assault, he eventually caught the tail end of a disdainful look from Dalton.

"You," he said slowly, "want to move to the woods?"

"The mountains, maybe. Nowhere too far."

As if Dalton psychically sensed the waiter on an approach pattern to their table, he waved him off.

"If these guys lock in on this site branding deal," he said, "you'd only have to come in two, three days a week. You could be on vacation half the time."

"I'm not interested in a vacation."

Dalton slammed his fist down. "I call bullshit," he said. "You're a fool to say no to this."

Luke's agent leaned back in his chair and peered through his designer sunglasses at a woman walking by, not failing to recognize her blouse was at least a size too small. Discouraged by the rapidly fraying conversation at hand, Dalton grabbed a smartphone out of his pocket, scanned it for signs of life, and set it neatly next to his drink.

"Even a tenth of the advance we got for *The Dweeb King TV Guide* would be enough to get me through six months," Luke said. "They'd agree to that, don't you think?"

"What is so burning that you must express yourself this very instant, anyway?"

Luke ignored this. "Clyde can lead the site team, and Shelton is all set to take over for me."

"Now I know you're shitting me. You hate Shelton."

"He writes most of my feed as it is."

"I make it a habit not to question my clients' artistic drives," Dalton said. "But you need to turn this train around."

"I gave my super thirty days' notice this morning," Luke said.

Dalton reached for his billfold, making a bold signal that their rendezvous had come to an end. "Without mentioning anything to me."

"You'd have told me not to do it," Luke replied.

Dalton set out a twenty and finished his coffee.

"I'll cover early costs out of pocket and use the advance for the rest," Luke said.

"I don't know what kind of cloud has gotten in your way here. You'll torpedo your career."

"I can always reclaim my Dweeb throne in six months if it all falls apart."

"This deal will not be available in six months," Dalton said. "It's available now."

"I don't want your deal," Luke replied, smiling. "I want my own."

Dalton got up to leave. "For the record," he said, "if we weren't friends, I would have fired you today."

"Noted," Luke replied.

3

Luke spent the last weekend of September streamlining his Tribeca apartment, deciding what he'd need for his journey into rural splendor and what was to be sent off storage. Kitchenware and most of his clothing were indiscriminately thrown into large boxes (often mixed haphazardly), but when it came to Luke's movies, books, and other treasured pop culture trinkets, he considered each knickknack with a museum curator's attention to detail.

In the days leading up to this move-out afternoon, he'd cataloged every piece of etcetera in the place, recalling precisely how he convinced Loretta Lee to autograph his press pass after a concert in Nashville, but forgetting which of his Dweeb King pals tracked down a pack of matches from the Railroad Diner set in *Northwest Passage* for him. Luke even found himself waxing nostalgic about not only where the first woman he slept with on his once-brand-new couch was today, but what the hell her first name was.

Alas, Luke had no time for strolls down memory lane. His 1992 Jeep Cherokee was double-parked in front of his building on Grand Street, and the car horn honks and screeching brakes the jalopy continuously provoked forced him to stay in business mode. He triple-checked closet shelves, made sure the oven was off, left the key under the mat for the maid, and went on his way.

Luke's beloved ride, The B-Town Bitch, was not a city vehicle, which was fine since the ol' girl hardly ever came into NYC, there being more than enough space for her at Luke's parents' place in Altoona, a couple of hours away.

Pam Sullivan hated the rustbucket, feeling that her son,

ostensibly a successful television personality, shouldn't be driving a car whose bazooka-blasting muffler signaled her smoky approach from a mile away, but Luke's dad shared his son's affinity for the clunker. He persuaded his wife to allow B-Town to reside at the (mostly hidden) far end of their driveway.

Dalton had soberly reminded Luke on multiple occasions that a first-time novelist without a bankable concept didn't deserve an advance at all, but thanks to those stupid best-selling reference tomes from Luke and his Dweeb King cronies, his publishers had made a pretty penny off a relatively minor investment. This allowed Dalton an opportunity to glad-hand his way to contracting a menial chunk of change for his client, now a fledgling literary fiction writer.

Luke originally thought a funky skiing pocket in Vermont might make a perfect novelist's destination, but this alpine fantasia was cut off at the knees right away. Dalton had his assistants plan out a budget for the author-dork (minus his fifteen percent, of course), and it was determined that high-profile East Coast burgs were cost-prohibitive.

Luke would have to head inland.

Dalton set him up with a two-room cabin in Deer Meadow, West Virginia, deep in the Allegheny Mountains, a six-hour drive from New York City. As part of his arrangement with his website (and Dalton, for that matter), Luke had to check in with Dweeb King once a week, so as long as his bachelor pad came with basic electricity and an internet connection, he was good to go.

Luke planned a three-day travel cycle from Gotham to West Virginia, with stop number one being a proper visit with the parents in Pennsylvania. During the previous day's B-Town retrieval, Luke had been too busy to amble down Main Street and consider his old stomping grounds, and as he did this now, he felt a creeping, bitter dread.

In Altoona, you had to brace yourself for incestuous familiarity: it was a big enough town that not everyone recognized you, but folks who did were likely to have an encyclopedic knowledge of your biography, skeletons and all.

Truth be told, Luke was a little more recognizable than most Blair County residents, even as a kid. Inspired by the popular movie review program *Gene and Dean* that aired on his local PBS affiliate in the late 1980s, Luke successfully petitioned his town paper to sign him on as a weekly movie critic – call him the Dweeb Prince, perhaps.

Luke at the Movies was a non-paying gig, but it brought with it an *Altoona Bee* staff ID card that admitted Luke into the State Theater for free, a laminated badge that was for many years his most prized possession.

He passed that cinema he used to frequent twice a week in the September dusk, though now it was just one more of the town's many antique stores. *The Bee* itself had also gone out of business, thanks in no small part, from his dad's vantage point, to Luke and *his* internet bullying print media out of commission.

The Sullivan homestead was not only cleaner than it was when Luke and his brothers were young, it was fancier. As Sullivan sons went off to college and established homes of their own, Pam staged an extensive, ever-evolving renovation, updating the house with the sleekest modern appliances, tiling, and furniture her pocketbook could handle.

Intent on preserving this newness, and knowing full well Luke's penchant for klutziness, Kyle said to his son upon pouring him half a glass of red wine, "Don't spill it."

Luke begrudgingly heeded the warning and steered clear of the new carpet in the living room.

If you were to look at the three of them settling in for their meal, you'd acknowledge that Luke was undeniably his parents' son. Kyle and Luke both showcased common stocky, slightly hunched-over builds, and Luke and his mom had unmistakably similar faces, though Luke never smiled as widely as Pam did, being overly conscious of the space between his front teeth that Altoona's finest orthodontist wasn't able to minimize back in his *Luke at the Movies* days.

Moving a napkin to her lap, Pam asked, "Again, where is this new apartment?"

Luke remembered the value of keeping things short and sweet during Sullivan inquisitions. Considering his parents' double-barrel stares, he said, "It's a cabin. In West Virginia."

"What's in West Virginia?" Kyle asked.

"Peace and quiet, I hope."

"Can I ask how you can afford this?" Pam added, dripping with maternal skepticism.

"You didn't come here to borrow money, did you?" his dad asked.

The interrogation continued, but Luke didn't break the seal on the full impetus behind his sojourn to Deer Meadow. His parents were interested in what he had up his sleeve, but being well-mannered WASPs, they fell in line with an implicit protocol to wait for information to be broadcast rather than aggressively chase it down, and Luke wasn't offering full disclosure.

After a dinner spent gossiping about his brothers and their kids, Luke prompted his dad: "Should we see if the baseball game taped?"

Luke peeked up at the moon slowly inching across the sky from the twin bed in his childhood bedroom. At one time, this set of walls had provided him private adolescent sanctuary, but now, with its fresh linens and homely, respectable furniture, it might as well have been a hotel single.

He found the stillness of Altoona unsettling. With the chores and legwork of the day, Luke had steadfastly been able to maintain a sturdy reserve, but here in the quiet of this prosaic alien kingdom that was once his, each fleeting tendril of thought he conjured found its end in discord, a question mark.

Twenty years ago he'd have put headphones on and let rock and roll drown out these circling ruminations. Tonight, though, he stared at the moon, biting his fingernails, waiting for dreams to compel his eyes to close.

4

Most babies didn't care much for Luke. He was capable of changing a diaper and had a clean track record as far as preventing micro-persons under his care from, you know, being abducted by aliens or falling into vats of boiling acid, but as a rule, young humans were not typically drawn to him.

Luke's best friend Ray Powell and his wife, Nicole, were sure this toddler distrust was tied innately to Luke's long-standing and adamant rule to never baby talk with anyone, bambinos or otherwise.

When Ray's daughter Lori was born, on one of the hottest July Wednesdays Altoona had seen in decades, Luke made a point of being among the first to meet the new arrival. After congratulating the exhausted couple in their cramped hospital room, Luke held the little meatloaf in his arms and found himself awash with a sense of connection between the two of them, cultivating an instant kinship he frankly hadn't felt with his biological nephews.

But when Nicole witnessed the purposefully adult inflection Luke used when he spoke to Lori, she was put off by it, finding it aloof and detached, almost mean. It wasn't until Lori turned three, when the Powells came to the Big Apple for a getaway, that Nicole learned the odd value of Luke's approach.

They planned a double date with college chums of Nicole's and enlisted Luke as big-city babysitter. Luke was initially astonished at the sheer volume of toys, books, and baby infrastructure that had to be hauled in to facilitate Lori's stay in his small apartment, but as the night progressed and the kid remained consistently occupied with her complex matrix of playthings, he understood their indispensability.

The next morning, Nicole and Ray returned to Tribeca and began the intricate ballet of moving Lori's accessories back into their SUV. Luke insisted on helping them lug the paraphernalia down the four flights of his building's narrow stairs, but seeing as they were in a rush, Nicole assured him he'd be most helpful staying in the apartment with the kid.

Without Lori's gear available to her, Luke's babysitting mojo evaporated. She stared him down, teetering between lazy contentment and outright conniption.

Luke looked around at the collectible superhero action figures and space alien telephones that took up every square inch of shelf space in his dork dormitory, but none of it would hold much use as entertainment to a bored child. Luke believed Lori knew this, too – the face she had fixed on him was a come-on, a quiet urge compelling him to rise to the daunting task of amusing her.

They stood in this standoff for a while, until Luke spotted one of his many bookshelves jam-packed with vinyl LPs. In a frantic attempt to divert a meltdown, he set five of them on the floor in front of the kid.

What followed would later play out in Luke's mind as a perfectly-honed *cool uncle* rock and roll fable, the kind of story he could tell at Lori's college graduation party that'd make both of them sound maximally bad-ass.

Luke explained in supergeek detail why the shiny prog-rock albums before Lori were of such urgent musical relevance. Luke doubted she gave a rip about the underrated synth arrangements on "Blue Sweetheart" from side two of *Papa Thunder* by Smokey Coloma and the Cougar Fighters, but the tactile fun of the black discs on display drew her attention all the same.

Luke grabbed other LPs, showing off spinning sleeve inserts, trippy container-within-container graphic designs, and memento photo inserts of various sizes and shapes. Lori was pop-eyed with awe, as attentive to these albums as she had been to the trinkets she'd occupied herself with twelve hours earlier.

When Ray and Nicole saw this, they locked and loaded their cellphone cameras on instinct, capturing Uncle Luke instructing their three-year-old how to chant *"ARE YOU READY TO ROCK?"* with appropriate rock and roll rasp.

Luke was so lost in this remembrance that when he knocked at Ray and Nicole's front door, he didn't notice the fleet of cars parked outside the family's large home. As Ray led him inside, Luke saw this was no casual Monday evening at the Powell house.

Children dressed in formalwear (and the occasional fairy princess costume) bounced down the hall toward playrooms out of sight. Women transported trays of food into and out of the kitchen. Men drank beer and chatted quietly near the living room television set.

Luke was never particularly comfortable at social events, especially ones he wasn't expecting, but it always felt good to see Ray's face. The two of them had been misfit cousins since the fourth grade, and while Ray stayed close to home and became a well-rounded family man as Luke ventured off to conquer the jungles of New York City, their rapport never waned. Squeezing his shoulder, Luke offered Ray his requisite bag of DVDs that had been sent to Dweeb King offices for review.

As he inspected them, Ray exclaimed, "Oh, man. This one doesn't come out for a month! Nice!"

When Nicole saw Luke, she lit up ("BFF!" she screamed) and skipped toward him for a warm embrace. Blonde and comely, she struck Luke as exotically athletic, as if she were an Olympic swimmer from Europe with a dark past. Such illusions were shattered, however, whenever Nicole spoke: New Yawk all the way.

Nicole recapped the week's notable Altoona gossip as

Luke watched her mom walk through the kitchen holding Lori. Yana was a thin wisp of a woman with an accent that bore distinct Russian gravel.

Her singular battle in the Powell family structure concerned her not being content with the *grandma* and *grandpa* monikers Ray's parents held, instead insisting young Lori adopt *babulya* and *dedulya* for her and Nicole's dad in noble Moscow tradition.

She gestured to Ray's younger brother and said to Lori, "Who's that? Is that Uncle Travis?"

Nicole nodded. Yana then pointed at herself. "Who is this?"

"Grandma!"

"No. Babulya. *Babulya.*"

They entered the living room, and Yana's spirits sagged. "Ah," she said. "The godfather."

The disdain in Yana's eyes was in response to what inevitably would occur at this stage of Luke's introduction.

Rubbing salt in an open wound, Yana looked to Lori and asked, "Who's that?"

The kid locked her big brown eyes on him. "Uncle Luke! *ARE YOU READY TO ROCK?*"

Ray's sister made a loud, avian screech, and spoke quickly, like she couldn't get the words out fast enough. "She did it again!" she said. "How cute!"

Yana turned Lori toward another section of the room, restarting her *babulya* speech drill, hoping for better results. Luke patted the kid's arm as she was carried away.

Nicole elbowed Luke in the side playfully. "You need a drink," she said.

5

After a few hours driving down winding highways through sleepy towns with opulent Indian Casinos where their personalities might once have been, Luke's eyes widened as the last fifty miles into Deer Meadow took B-Town up a steady, sharp grade. The greenery around him became dense and lush, and giant rock formations jutted up out of the ground, veritable mountains of their own.

Luke kept B-Town's stereo at full volume on this expedition, not on account of any musical craving, but because he needed something to drown out the car's squeaks, scrapes, and general engine disharmony. Once they were near town, though, Luke braved the atonal orchestra and switched the radio off.

He first marveled at Deer Meadow's trees, which towered high above the road. Verdant woodlands served as backdrops to gas stations and mom-and-pop stores on the main drag. As Luke passed a sign officially proclaiming city limits, he flitted through the sandwich wrappers and soda bottles on his passenger seat, grasping for the map Dalton printed out for him.

Luke rejected the idea of using his smartphone to find his way: ink and paper worked fine, thank you very much, as long as he could find the damned thing.

The place was deserted. Its uninhabited structures – a restaurant, a post office, a shoebox movie theater – offered no proof that humans actually resided there. Luke rolled down B-Town's driver-side window and thrilled to the temperature drop. An hour ago, he'd been lamenting his car's air conditioning weakness, but the breeze in Deer Meadow had a cool kick to it that defied the Indian summer he'd left behind in Pennsylvania.

There were enormous empty residences up off the highway. Outdoor tables on decks were locked down with tarps, and well-maintained driveways were entirely free of vehicles. Luke had heard from one of Dalton's assistants that the town wasn't far from a popular ski resort, but it appeared that during the current off-season, he'd have the village to himself.

Luke's cabin was separated from other lots on its cul-de-sac, nestled among hedges and overgrown fences. He looked at the homes across the way, and though the sunshine was bright upon them, they seemed mysteriously threatening. In keeping with whatever zombie apocalypse had purged Deer Meadow of its population, nearly all of them were unoccupied.

In his rental, there were two rooms downstairs, one with a chunky wooden desk in its corner, another housing a bed and a dresser. The bathroom was in need of a good scrubbing, but compared to most restrooms in New York, it was a sparkling gem.

Stale dust permeated the second floor. Luke made note of a retro sofa, a coffee table with decades-old magazines in its lower compartments, and mirrors on every wall, each large plane lacquered with embossed bronze textures, lending the room a kaleidoscopic blur, even in the dark.

The rickety TV had to go, however. You could take the Dweeb King out of the city, but Luke would be damned if he'd watch his beloved Cornerstone Standard DVDs on such a rustic machine.

He took a deep breath and yanked the cord to the drapes that shielded the Miss Havisham Experience from the outside world and saw… nothing, really. As he stepped onto the cabin's small balcony, Luke noted below him, in ample supply, dirt. His backyard was abandoned fare, lumpy soil peppered with the occasional non-exotic weed.

He thought he heard a car drive by and was excited to spot his first town denizen, but it was only B-Town's loose hubcap falling off and jingling on the pavement.

6

Instead of indulging a compulsive instinct to unpack and arrange his new place with deranged specificity, Luke left all boxes but one in his mudroom and bounded upstairs. He poured a mug of the cheap wine he stocked up on while passing through Altoona and placed a package labeled *Manuscripts* on his living room coffee table.

Here was his archive: ideas, outlines, and drafts Luke had amassed since adolescence. He had, after all, officially embarked upon the most artistic endeavor of his career, and he figured an appropriate place to start was a retrospective check to see if he had material in his arsenal that might provide a stable foundation for the novel he was about to begin.

At the top of the heap was a screenplay he worked on with his nemesis, Matt Shelton. A longtime Dweeb King contributor (and as of several days earlier, its new president), Shelton had never been a dear friend of Luke's, but as their freshman dorm's two most outspoken resident movie buffs, they forged a cinephilic association that over time evolved into Dweeb King's pop culture enterprise.

Shelton, a squat and impish fellow, claimed to be peri-
lously allergic to cigarette smoke (believable, sure) as well as
certain types of body odor (bullshit). These restrictions kept
him out of cinemas and most public places, which motivat-
ed him to establish and maintain a state-of-the-art home
theater in his basement. Shelton was machine guru supreme
at Dweeb King, and his technical fluency was a valuable
counterweight to Luke's free-wheeling takes on movies.

Shelton originally had the idea to collaborate, hoping
their volatile way of working each other into cinematic fren-
zies could be translated into original prose. The result of
their two weeks of screenwriting was *The Haggard Usher,* a
thriller about a detective whose years of drug abuse threat-
ens to jeopardize a high-profile murder case he's commis-
sioned by a trampy brunette to solve.

It was painfully clear to Luke which scenes were his.
Shelton's scenery descriptions and detailed analyses of character motivations droned on endlessly, while Luke's dia-
logue-heavy entries were exasperating rip-offs of popular
films he'd watched during his college years.

As he and Shelton agreed years ago, this one would
continue to gather dust.

Next was the outline of a space drama Luke had concocted for a junior year screenwriting class. At the time of
its assignment, he had been in the throes of a stifling case of
writer's block, and when prompted for advice about how to
kick it, his roommate insisted that Luke get stoned and *ride
the lightning.*

There just so happened to be a joint nearby.

In his haze, Luke forgot to set his alarm, and he nearly
slept through his morning class. It wasn't until he was halfway across campus that he bothered to look at the product

of his marijuana-enhanced expedition.

Not recalling specifics from the psychedelic night before, Luke was mortified when he flipped to the first page of *Spacetime Immigrants*, a sci-fi saga (the first in a set of two trilogies, naturally) featuring Nordic biker nymphets and the extraterrestrial sock puppets who love them.

Thankfully, Luke didn't have to read this in front of his peers. He tucked it back into his knapsack and enlisted his roommate to drop the assignment off for him. He ended up getting a B, though his teacher wrote on its cover that it needed *a little finessing*.

In a fairer world, the misfired folly of *Spacetime Immigrants* would be a worst-case scenario for a writer assessing the horrors of his artistic past, but in Luke's case, this was not to be.

Here was *Licorice Dakota*.

Luke's first finished full-length script was a romance inspired by the love affair the author had with Roberta Davis, a four-month relationship that involved enthusiastic, youthful fornication, emotional late-night poetry reading, and a road trip that ended in a car crash and a weepy break-up.

In *Licorice Dakota*, Luke and Roberta avatars drive around while listening to music that *speaks to them* and repeatedly make in-jokes about facets of their collective ennui they find hilarious. Luke brushed through this, wincing at the abominations each page brought.

Waitresses look at 'Ron' and are "compelled to make love to him on the spot." 'Amanda' at one point opines, through waves of tears, "This situation of ours is totally out of *trol!*"

Trol, of course, was a colloquialism shortening the word *control* that Luke and Roberta once thought was a significant addition to formal English slang.

Both lead characters also use the word *hecka* often, a term invented as a revolt against hipsters who had co-opted *hella* as the euphemism of the moment. The last exchange Luke read before looking up from *Licorice Dakota* was:

> RON: I love you.
> AMANDA: But do you *hecka* love me?

Luke held up the 250-page script, noting that, if produced, it would be a four-hour finished film, and grumbled at its pretentious bloat. He then regarded his crackling fireplace and knew it'd make a great final resting place. Luke kept the title page but tossed the rest of *Licorice Dakota* into its funeral pyre, content that he'd prevented the world from ever having to encounter the nightmarish doorstopper.

Luke refilled his wine mug and continued his mission, pulling up another script: *Art in the Scarehaus.* That's right – the haunted mansion at the center of Luke's horror story was so chilling it was pronounced with a German accent.

Oh, boy, he thought.

7

His introduction to Keene's, Deer Meadow's only restaurant, began with a brassy bartender screaming, "Oh my God! You're from the TV!"

In New York, Luke's low-rent celebrity status inspired reaction like this once or twice a week. If he thought his

stint in the boonies would bring him anonymity, this out-
burst proved otherwise.

The place had an overstuffed appeal, with blinking
lights on the ceiling almost outshining the patterned glow of
the video poker machines built into its horseshoe bar.

The woman who reacted to him so emphatically pointed a finger at Luke as he found his way to a stool, as though
there was a follow-up to her initial rant that wasn't quite
coming to her. She was tall and voluptuous, dressed in a
yellow t-shirt and jean shorts the gray-haired guy sitting
across from Luke studied intently.

In an attempt to jumpstart the conversation, Luke said,
"There are people in this town! You're the first I've seen."

The woman allowed Luke a goofy smile. "We're like a
bad case of the crabs," she said. "You think we're gone,
then we pop right back up again."

She hesitated. "But seriously – you're on TV."

Speaking the way he always did on the subject, Luke
said, "I have made a living on television, yes."

He did a quick survey of the room, observing five
groups of diners and a trio of whispering women huddled in
one of the establishment's dark booths.

"What are we drinking?" the bartender asked.

"What vodkas do you have?"

She gave Luke a condescending look. "New York or
Boston?" she asked. "New York, right?"

Luke nodded.

"Here at Keene's, it's all well all the time," she said. "It's
how we keep our overhead – and your prices – so low."

"What would you recommend for a new local?"

"New local?" she asked. "I'd have bet my husband's
balls you were just passing through."

"Moved into town yesterday," he said.

She grabbed a can of beer from a small refrigerator and spun it down the bar toward Luke. She then wiped her hands on her trusty bar towel and extended him a courteous hand.

"I ask a lot of personal questions, but also have a bad habit of letting my victims drink on the house," she said. "They call me Misty."

"Luke," he replied. Misty had been hoping a first name would be enough to prompt recognition. Helping her out, her new customer added, "Luke Sullivan."

Even the recitation of his full name didn't do it. "From *Entertainment Talk*."

A petite woman playing video poker solved the mystery. "You're the nerd!"

Misty covered her eyes, grumbling. "I knew that!" she exclaimed. "Yeah, I saw your bit a few times."

"What, you stopped watching?"

"Pete and I only do reality shows now," Misty said. "I want backstabbing housewife bitches and duck hunters building stinky yurts on deserted islands. Anything with information or a plot, and I'm out. I don't have the time."

The poker player, who Luke would soon learn was named Donna, glanced at him quizzically. "I never understood you, anyway," she said. "Why would anybody *want* to be a nerd?"

"*Dweeb* is our preferred brand," Luke said with press conference sterility. "I like to say that a dweeb has a true dedication about what he's interested in, whereas a nerd is more of a…"

He didn't finish. Misty screeched: "ARE WE GOING TO BE ON TV?"

Schizophrenically, she calmed and swiveled toward Donna. "You know who would be a great dweeb? Kristina's boyfriend."

Donna returned to her game. "I don't understand a word he says."

Misty scanned her bar until she found a dark-eyed, dangerously skinny woman sipping a drink with a straw. Misty banged a plastic cup against the counter, making a good deal of noise.

The woman heeded Misty's alarm call, and the bartender loudly asked, "Is that guy here? Your beau?"

This Kristina person Misty was speaking to immediately rubbed Luke the wrong way. Her harsh, stumped face snarled as she blinked twice (slowly, for some reason), and spoke as though she was a double agent in a spy movie.

"He is smoking," she said, a steely accent refining her already astringent aura.

Misty banged her cup again, this time in the direction of a passing waitress. "Go bring in Kristina's fella," Misty said. "He'll love the new guy."

Luke chose not to partake in the video poker that had four Keene's patrons crouched over the bar, intent on winning pixelated fortunes. He was doing his best to finish the second lukewarm beer Misty served him when a figure strode Luke's way with dramatic gravity. The lack of light in the place accentuated the man's stark facial features and debonair suit.

His hand hit Luke's intently. "I am Marion," he said. "I admire your work."

"I admire your accents," Luke responded. "I had no idea Deer Meadow was so exotic."

Misty, not exactly eavesdropping behind them, added,

"You can't spit in this town without hitting a Romanian these days. There are, what, thirty of you guys here?"

Marion set a grotesque black cocktail on the counter. "About that, yes," he said as he pulled out the stool next to Luke. "I buy a round for you, Mr. Sullivan."

"I was just about to head home."

Misty blocked this by setting a new can of beer in front of him.

"Tell me how Dweeb King from TV comes to West Virginia."

"I am no longer the Dweeb King," Luke drearily said. "They announce my replacement on Monday's show."

"Why stop?"

He shrugged as the three sirens from the rearmost Keene's booth passed by, cooing to Marion in foreign whispers. Luke leaned toward his new friend after they left and asked, "Who are these beautiful women?"

"Romanians. Not a dog in the bunch."

"Evidently," Luke said with a sigh, choosing not to consider Marion's companion in this assessment.

"They know nothing about movies, though," Marion said. "No Romanian woman likes good cinema. Everything has to be dumb and in English. You and Marion, though. The two of us discuss very important movies. Films, Dweeb King. Films."

"Call me Luke."

"I am an artist, as well, you know."

"Yeah?"

"I will run a wedding video business one day," he said. "It has been a dream for many years."

"What do you do out here?"

"We all work at the casino," Marion said. "Do you play cards?"

"Nah."

Kristina approached Marion. He turned toward her and cradled her forearm gingerly. Luke thought it might be the beer, but the way she looked, especially up close, was genuinely menacing.

Thankfully, Marion didn't feel the need to introduce her. The Romanian stood up and took a cigarette out of his shirt pocket.

He said quietly to Luke, "I can help with women. Let's talk soon."

Marion bounded outside, chasing his gargoyle to whatever rendezvous she had planned.

Luke noticed that Marion wore shoes with giant lifts in them. Maybe it was a Romanian thing.

8

Luke didn't detect clouds gathering outside as he began unpacking his last box, one marked *Cornerstone Standard*. These DVDs and Blu-rays were precious physical properties, and Luke insisted on handling and organizing them carefully.

In his years writing for Dweeb King, Luke had been such a staunch supporter of the New York-based company that he'd been put on what his Cornerstone liaison Kevin Turney called their *Send All* list, meaning whenever CS had a new title hitting the market, Luke received an early review copy, which allowed him to galley up an expansive array of discs.

Any misgivings Luke had about working on a gabbing dipshit pop culture program like *Entertainment Talk* were countered by his work with Cornerstone, whose cause he was always striving to highlight. It wasn't an easy sell convincing producers to devote air time to a studio that specialized in old, rare, and mostly foreign-language movies, but in character as Dweeb King, Luke had been able to focus at least one story a month on Cornerstone and their inimitable body of work, which brought him a bookish pride.

Luke had an exhaustive knowledge of Cornerstone's lineage, its early days selling LaserDiscs, and its years before that as an influential distributor in the 1950s and 60s that introduced the world to Gunner Hedlund, Angelo Ricci, and countless other internationally renowned filmmakers.

Peering over editions of these cinematic landmarks as he strategically placed them on his shelf, Luke felt the smoothness of their cases, opening them and leafing through the smartly-versed booklet essays that accompanied each release. On their rear faces were short synopses of the films as well as lists of documentaries and commentary tracks from scholars and fellow directors that supplemented the historical imperatives of the movies with lucid, academic clarity.

The snippet of Cornerstone's mission statement that graced the top back corner of all discs was (as Luke could recite on cue): "Cornerstone Standard, an evolving collection of diverse masterworks from around the globe, presents…" There was a preening pretense to the ardor of his appreciation for the studio, he had to admit, but Luke was happy to wear his affected adoration proudly.

Luke worked on this Cornerstone project through the afternoon. *Regular* movies and books were arranged alphabetically, like riff-raff. Cornerstone branded its editions with unique spine numbers, benchmarks of the order in which each film was prepared for its respective format. This was a codification Luke liked to base his beloved treasury upon. Denis Fontaine's *Time's Façade* (CS#1) was the first Cornerstone DVD ever distributed, so it sat in pole position on the left edge of Luke's main shelf, and hundreds of successive titles fell into place judiciously behind it.

He picked up his Cornerstone Standard coffee mug (he owned two) after straightening out the final Blu-ray of his collection, and surveyed his achievements.

It was official: Luke Sullivan lived here.

Having completed every chore Luke could think of that was associated with the move, he knew it was time to write. The downstairs office was purposely stark, free of potential diversion. Luke's laptop was so old it wasn't capable of connecting to the internet, and was boosted up on both sides by a pair of inch-wide books.

The machine was so prone to overheating that if it didn't have generous airflow beneath it, it would turn hot to the touch and shut down noisily in protest. This threat of impending doom functioned as a useful catalyst for Luke's work ethic – realizing his work could turn to dust at any moment implored him to type fast and save often.

He set a stack of yellow notepads and a pen on the desk next to the computer and proceeded to stare at his blank screen, biting his nails compulsively. After ten minutes of this, he'd managed to draw blood from one of his cuticles, which prompted a bandage break.

Extending this timeout, Luke paced, drank more coffee, and ultimately procrastinated for more than an hour before typing in a bold font, "CHAPTER ONE."

He heard wind.

Luke hopped up the stairs. The tempest outside was compelling trees to sway violently, leaves and stray pieces of nature churning around them with rushing speed. One ferocious gale boomed through the forest and hit the cabin, causing all lights and freshly-dusted appliances in the place to zap to black.

The intensity of this weather made Luke tremble with city-boy dread, but now an orphan of the storm, he had to admit it felt great knowing that fucking writing computer was off.

9

"The dweeb is back!"

Peppered by flecks of newly fallen snow, Luke shook off his sock hat. "Somebody turned the weather on," he said.

Misty thrust dirty glasses into a sink and scrubbed them rapidly. Luke sat at what he decided he'd call *his* stool near her, noting the place was crammed with diners.

"Ski season is coming," she said. "I give it two more weeks before the first blizzard hits. What are we drinking?"

Luke grabbed a menu, knowing if he didn't get something to eat, dinner would be trail mix and wine back at the cabin, and he had that for lunch. Misty interrupted his perusal by gingerly placing a neon blue drink in front of him. The poker machine beneath it infused the concoction with an otherworldly glow.

"We call it an Alabama Headache," Misty said. "A Keene's original. Courtesy of this gentleman." She saluted to a bearded fellow wearing red plaid, who lifted a blue libation of his own in recognition.

"People are interested in Deer Meadow's newest celebrity," Misty said. "Let's get to know each other!"

Luke considered avenues of backtrack but knew which way the wind was blowing. "Best to give in to the Cougars of Keene's," Misty said, sensing his resistance.

Slapping his menu on the bar, Luke picked up his Alabama Headache. "Fire away," he said.

Misty wiped off her hands excitedly. Half the folks at the bar turned toward her. "The actor – the one from the car-racing movie," the bartender said with schoolgirl enthusiasm. "Is it true he…?"

Luke choked back a sip of Headache. "No tabloid stuff. I don't do that."

The crowd whined in objection, many of them electing to return to the conversations they were having before Luke arrived. He turned toward the gentleman who bought him his drink.

"Alabama Headache," Luke said. "Hit me."

"What's a TV guy doing in Deer Meadow?"

"I'm writing a book."

"What kind?" Misty asked. "One about dweebs?"

A faceless voice chimed in from across the bar. "Didn't you already do that?"

"We put out a pop culture guide last year, yeah," he said. "Has anybody read it?"

In an attempt to break the silence this question inspired, Luke added, "Does Dear Meadow even have a book store?"

The lesson learned by Luke on this blustery evening was to avoid Alabama Headaches forever. Plus, he forgot to order food, so once the man who introduced Luke to the blue terrors moved closer and they continued, for some distressing reason, to order round after round of the toxic cocktails, the abominable moonshine began taking its Satanic effect on Luke's empty stomach.

Normally, after four or five drinks, Luke would be a goner, sleepy and intent on finding a snug place to pass out. If the party was enjoyable enough to impel him to keep at it, however, he was known to experience a Jekyll/Hyde switch, transmogrifying into who Dalton nicknamed Blotto.

When Blotto took Luke's human form, he showcased an exuberant raucousness, often dancing feverishly and singing songs (mostly unspeakably filthy rap favorites) at excessive volumes.

Luke would ceremonially wake up the next morning with a tectonic hangover whenever Blotto came to town, but he'd have zero recollection of the night before, as if his intoxicated doppelgänger had an ability to turn off Luke's short-term memory entirely.

The morning after his evening at Keene's, Luke was able to (barely) recall the following foggy moments:

• At one point, he stole his new buddy's stocking cap and wore it himself. When the man said his name was Guy Pollock, Luke flatly dismissed such a notion, insisting that Alabama Headache was a better moniker for him.

- He asked a woman at the bar what her favorite book was, and she had trouble picking one, ultimately confessing that the recipes her great-great-aunt had collected in the early 1900s were what she read most often. Luke's response to this was: "THAT'S THE PERFECT ANSWER!"

Blotto's activities in addition to these (that conscious Luke was unable to access):

- He gave a ten-minute lecture about Cornerstone Standard, and no one in the establishment cared.
- Misty snapped a series of photographs with her smartphone throughout the evening. Every time he knew he was getting his picture taken, Blotto would flip Misty the bird and open his mouth. Blotto's eyes were not open in these pictures.
- Around midnight, Blotto opened the front door and screamed into the wind, "WHERE ARE MY ROMANIANS?"

10

He opened his eyes. There was *way* too much light in his living room. The television blared static loudly, and once Luke made the terrible mistake of sitting up, it was clear that every lamp and fixture in the room was ablaze, the cabin's power fully regained.

As Luke threw off a dusty couch blanket, he saw that while he had stripped his bottom half down to his boxers, from the waist up, he still wore his down jacket, a sweater, and a t-shirt underneath that.

Trail mix littered the ground in messy, congealed clumps.

Luke tried to get a concrete grasp on the morning, attempting routine duties of the day, but after half a cup of coffee and twenty minutes of inert staring at his laptop, he pulled the living room blinds closed again and returned to the couch.

He laid still, firmly burrito-ed in a warm blanket. He wasn't necessarily sleepy – it was more a case of immobile disquiet, a state of anxious catatonia. He had a bad feeling the post-Blotto hangover currently in the process of super-nova within his cranium wouldn't subside until one more night's sleep was under his belt, which meant there was nothing to do but soldier through daylight hours.

Here was a twinge of guilt, too. Luke likely wouldn't write anything that day. He quietly brokered a deal with himself (*Write twice as much tomorrow to make up for it*, he thought), but knew he'd find a way to shimmy out of that arrangement somehow. Right now he needed comfort, and that was most efficiently accomplished by looking at his

Cornerstone shelf.

He could make out the CS logos on the spines of the company's recently-released titles and marveled in their elegance. He recalled that Dweeb King helped break the story of their updated insignia two years back, which prompted even more fervent fans than Luke to get tattoos of the new logo.

Once Luke had attempted to memorize all titles in the collection, but he never got far. The first three were easy: *Time's Façade* (CS#1), *Ancestry of Battle* (CS#2), *45 Lies* (CS#3). For a moment, not bothering to consider the other hundreds of titles under the Cornerstone banner, Luke thought about how much aesthetic weight this trio alone held. These were motion pictures of distinct noteworthiness, maybe not the three best movies of all time, but ones anomalous in their ability to instill wonder in audiences.

Luke suspended this rambling inner address, recognizing that an idea was percolating in an underground quadrant of his Alabama Headache-doused psyche. These Cornerstone films that served as such refreshing anodynes occupied an echelon that hovered above and beyond everyday cinema for him. Their elite distinction brought Luke a sense of pride, a surge of confidence as a consumer of art.

What would happen if he applied this highbrow concept to literature? Could this upend his dry spell? By rejecting humdrum media and applying Cornerstone's exclusively consequential ethic when considering what he'd consume, Luke could hone both his focus and his resolve, which might positively affect his prowess as a reader and, in turn, his basic shape as a writer.

Whether or not this *greatness begets greatness* philosophy was legitimate or an invitation to delusion, Luke decided in his ravaged state that he was going to unapologetically set out to make great art, an act that would be nurtured by only absorbing a literary diet of Cornerstone Standard caliber and stature.

Luke was so pleased with himself he was almost inspired to get back up and set upon his new task.

Almost.

11

Luke spent his lunch break the following day determining how to implement his freshly-invented literary exclusivity policy. He wanted a list that, like Cornerstone's, was intellectually responsible, but not irreducibly so. He craved a set of books that showcased both dramatic accomplishment and at least a modicum of genuine appeal.

Search engines kept suggesting an archive called The Modern Library 100. If the internet is to be believed, The ML100 came about when a collection of authorities in the literary world hammered out an inventory of the one hundred best novels written in English between 1900 and 1999. There was minor backlash hubbub in regards to the makeup of the selection committee and their choices, but compared to other resources Luke dug up, it stood tall.

Upon perusing the list in its entirety, Luke recognized he'd logged serious hours with many ML100 titles during his high school days, but he couldn't recall exact plot points from *A Passage to India*, and the only vague memories he could extract about *A Portrait of the Artist As a Young Man* was that stream of consciousness was involved.

His senior year English teacher, Ms. Linton, thought it was the best book ever written, whatever that was worth.

Seeing as Luke's inner bookworm had to act as disciplinarian in this undertaking, he decided on the spot that he couldn't pass off hazy remembrances of books he read twenty years ago as justifiable familiarity: he had to start from scratch.

Luke ported over information from the ML100 website and concocted a thorough spreadsheet. After printing a copy, he tracked down the Randolph County Library and drove the fifteen minutes to its nearest branch.

Finding the institution unsurprisingly vacant, Luke discussed his literary stratagem with a fair-haired sprite of a librarian named Crystal, who was thrilled to have a new task that did not involve reorganizing the library's Young Adult section (rampant teenage interest in vampire romance fiction left the area in a perpetual state of disarray).

Luke returned to his cabin with two grocery bags full of books. With leftover Cornerstone-organizing exactitude, he emptied a shelf near the kitchen and bit his nails, agonizing over whether to classify the books by title, author, or ML100 rank.

Without warning, the desktop computer in the living room assaulted him with an irritating string of beeps. Luke only used this machine for internet access, which, in addition to this new ML100 task, consisted of checking fantasy football stats and weather forecasts, as well as keeping up with Cornerstone Standard news (his handle in the online CS forum was Gus Van Cant, a spin on the director of CS#119).

When he tapped the thing to life, he initially didn't know how to track down the annoying pings. In fact, it was

all a bit Greek. Luke was intricately familiar with the idiosyncrasies of his fussy writing computer downstairs, but this
desktop — a tool Dalton's minions purchased and set up a
week before he headed to Deer Meadow — had applications
and add-ons Luke didn't understand. He attempted to iso-
late the noise, to decipher what program was burping, and
after closing browser windows dedicated to his ML100
business, he saw a small icon at the corner of his screen
blinking red.

Ray's name came into view, a message appearing beneath it: *Answer this immediately.*

Luke dragged his cursor over the program and the minute he did so, he saw a new line of text: *Hey, asshole!*

He hadn't brushed a key, yet Ray had pinpointed him
with Big Brother omniscience.

Luke typed: *Let me call you.*

The cursor flashed twice: *No can do. I'm at the office.*

Luke: *What's so important? Did you die?*

Ray: *I was supposed to ask you a month ago and forgot. We
want you to be godfather to baby number two.*

Luke paused, not sure why: *Yeah, of course. Got a name yet?*

Ray: *Nicole likes Deborah, but that makes me think of the red-
headed cheerleader from high school.*

Luke: *The one with the snaggletooth?*

Ray: *She had sweaty palms, too, right?*

Luke: *That's what I heard.*

Ray: *Just tell Nicole I asked you a month ago.*

Luke: *About the sweaty cheerleader?*

Ray: *Ha! How's the book coming?*

Luke sat back in his chair. Ray probably would buy any
bullshit he drummed up on the spot, but while Luke had no
reservations about playing fast and loose with the truth
when it came to his industry colleagues, he tried to maintain

as much integrity as he could with those closest to him. This virtue was in full bloom as Luke pulled the plug of the computer out of the wall, its screen diminishing instantly into nothing. He knew he'd get an earful from Ray about this when they talked next, but by then he might genuinely have progress to report.

He also determined his ML100 books should be organized by title.

Yeah, that was the way to go.

12

In the halcyon heyday of Dweeb King, a frequent topic of office conversation was Matt Shelton's wife. There was a stretch of time where Clyde, the site's well-dressed Chinese head programmer, thought she might not exist, but Luke claimed to have heard her voice on the telephone once, which was circumstantial enough to confirm her actuality to the guys.

It was fair to say that when it came to the Dweebs and Shelton, social circles didn't overlap. Shelton was the tapped-in computer geek Dweeb King couldn't thrive without, a key player in the company's hive of industry, but to a man, none of his co-workers could stand being around him, and this fueled endless hours of gossip about what poor soul hitched herself to him.

The Dweeb King guys were even known to quietly stare at Shelton for uncomfortably extensive periods of time.

Where typical cubicle employees might check emails, play with smartphones, or stare into space during workday downtime, *Shelton-viewing* was the default idling hobby for virtually everyone on their floor.

Clyde had a breakthrough while *Shelton-viewing* one dull spring day. He realized Shelton bore a striking resemblance to Kisser, the purple, human-sized walking eggplant with stubby legs from old fast food commercials. Clyde shared this discovery with the others, and Luke and his cronies marveled at his pitch-perfect deduction.

The Kisser Proclamation, as it would come to be known, inspired Dweeb King employees to *Shelton-view* whenever they could, and it all but threw gasoline on questions about the woman who married him. Clyde was convinced Shelton had an enormous monster dick, and that Kisser's wife was so hypnotized by his chimney cleaner (Clyde's preferred term) she was willing to look past the ear hair, the adult acne, and the breath – oh, sweet Jesus *the breath*.

Luke and his fellow Shelton-curious Dweeb Kings would often wonder over triple-beer lunches whether they were too harsh on the guy, but all of them could cite numerous examples of how horrible of a human being Shelton was. He was a congenial on-screen contributor during his *Entertainment Talk* segments – he was less rough around the edges than the others, for sure – but a Dweeb King employee stuck in anything more than basic conversation with the man would consider begging for a slow and painful death as an alternative.

Naively, Luke thought divorcing himself from the day-to-day business at the site would involve a clear, mundane changing of the guard, but Shelton balked at any such informality. Lawyers were called, arbitrations were scheduled, piles of paperwork presented themselves. What had once been a laid-back oasis for movie-crazy shut-ins became a *workplace*, a sterile corporate wasteland most Dweeb King officers avoided like the plague.

Luke secretly hoped Clyde would succeed him on his nerdy throne, but the guy's reluctance to get in front of a camera and his chronically undernourished productivity kept his name out of the hat (he was best left to hone his *Shelton-viewing* in his current position).

No one was surprised when Shelton was named head Dweeb. As loathed as he was, if Shelton were to quit, as he promised he would if he didn't get the promotion, they'd need to hire four people as his replacement, and no one wanted what would likely be a cut in pay as a result of that.

Once he took over, Kisser's designs for revamping the site seemed counterintuitive and far too heavy on home theater minutiae, which Clyde and Luke agreed was going to be challenging to overcome. Others had similar concerns, which is why Luke vowed to check in with Shelton once a week, on Friday mornings, to offer any advice or counsel he could to a company in a state of flux.

When Luke heard Kisser's nasal voice on his smartphone that first Friday in Deer Meadow, a familiar disquiet descended upon him. There was a silver lining, however. Shelton was never interested in casual pleasantries of any kind, so their chit-chat wouldn't last a nanosecond longer than it needed to.

He didn't even have an opportunity to say hello as Shelton drolly said, "Let's begin with the numbers."

When this dialogue came to an end, Luke got his agent on the horn.

"You're paranoid," Dalton said.

"He's going to run the place into the ground."

"Then that would be your penance for leaving the pop culture world, my friend," Dalton said. "Okay, we have real work to discuss."

"Weren't we just talking about work?"

"I had something delivered. Go check."

Luke set his coffee on the counter and opened his front door, realizing it was the first time he'd done that since waking up that morning. A package on the porch was addressed to him. After lugging it upstairs, Luke picked up his phone.

"Before you open it, I want to ask you a question," Dalton said.

"Shoot."

"How many times have I called you today?"

"I have no idea."

"I know you don't," Dalton said. "Five."

"I hate smartphones."

"I am the gateway to all money you stand to make while you whittle away in your little writing village."

"Your point?" Luke asked.

"There has to be a way for me to get in touch with you when I need to. Open your present."

Luke gleamed when he saw what was inside the box.

"Because you refuse to join the 21st-century world state, I have arranged for it to be installed tomorrow," Dalton said. "When this landline rings, you must answer. Day or night."

Luke pulled the object out of its case: a giant, shiny antique telephone, the sort you have to crank to use. He was so taken with the Northern Electric Candlestick that he hung up on Dalton and tested the toy's rotary dial.

He hardly noticed that Dalton kept calling him back on his smartphone, letting it vibrate on the counter as he pretended to be Jimmy Cagney barking orders at gangsters on his new gadget.

13

Its surface was riddled with the rigors of time, imperfections now canyons of precarious geography. Paint, wood, and texture collided in waves of ardent construction. Were those nail holes? What had been pinned there? Photos? Posters? Letters?

Luke read back what the early afternoon had inspired: an ode to the goddamned blank wall in front of him. He deleted the offending sequence. This marked the third straight day where nothing had progressed past seed phase. His sixth cup of coffee wasn't helping, either. Hastily considering reasons to leave the house, if only for a little while, he remembered he needed to mail his mom's birthday card. Sold.

The women at the Deer Meadow post office seemed hyper-human to Luke, as though they were animatronic robots on loan from a theme park. One was tall and frail, with frilly hair, and a dripping Massachusetts accent. Next to her was a matronly sweetheart whose laugh was so screamingly loud that no matter her conversational volume, when she'd chuckle, all customers in the room would flinch in response.

Engrossed in the regional character on display, Luke almost didn't sense something metallic jab him in the shoulder. He turned to see a patron ahead of him in line whose cane jutted out toward him. The old man gave Luke a look like maybe the prodding hadn't been an accident. He sure didn't bother with a smile.

"I need a form," he said with a husky voice.

Luke noted the man's dirty white t-shirt, tan shorts, and up-to-the-knee tube socks. "I need a *form*," he said again, louder.

Miss Robot Boston behind the counter yelled, "ROG-AH! Stop harassing customahs!"

"I need a mail hold form, and he's standing right in front of them."

Luke stepped aside, and Roger snatched a yellow paper from a case on the counter.

"Where ah you going, Rog-ah?"

"Got a doctor's appointment Friday," he said.

"You don't need a mail hold if you'ah only going to be gone for a few hou-ahs, Rog-ah."

The clerk next to her thunder-clapped another deafening whoop.

"You guys gum it up if I don't," Roger said. "I have checks coming in. I don't want anybody swiping them."

Luke had forgotten about the grouchy gentleman by the time he exited the post office, but there he was, lurking out side its front door. The man announced himself with a loud grunt, prompting Luke to stop dead in his tracks.

"What's your address?"

"Excuse me?"

"What's your *address?*" Roger sprang forward at him.

"Are you wincing at me?"

Luke, taken aback, said, "I'm not used to strangers asking me where I live."

"I don't shake hands, but if I did, this when I would do that," he said, taking a moment to stare at Luke blankly.

"I'm Roger. There. Now we're not strangers."

The old man leaned harder on his cane and said, "You either rented the old Freed place at 42 Roosevelt or you're in one of the Packard cabins up by the forest. Which is it?"

Hoping this exchange wouldn't end with him being murdered, Luke said, "By the woods. I just moved in."

"No shit. You're the writer. And you're out soaking up local color, stealing other people's words?"

"I wouldn't phrase it like that."

"Make sure you get it right, at least," Roger said, taking on an informational tone. "Naomi Sprout, the one with the laugh, is a born-again Christian, but she prefers *new to Jesus.*"

"And the lady with the accent?"

"We all have accents, boy," Roger said.

With a conniving twinkle in his eye, he added, "It'd be easier if you stopped by. I'll tell you the history of the whole damned place. If you're going to be here for a while, you should know who the big players are."

"That's kind of you, but…"

"From the Packard cabin, go to the southern end of the forest," Roger directed. "Mine's the A-frame with a hot tub out front. Tomorrow, four-ish. Bring beers."

14

His Wednesday writing jag was furiously energetic, but like so many of his first days in Deer Meadow, it came up empty. Luke had taught himself to type faster than ever, his coffee-fidget fingers racing about his keyboard, but as the sun set, Luke looked over the ten pages he'd produced, summarily wishing he hadn't. His main characters were inching toward credible establishment, but the voice wasn't there.

Screw it, he thought, running upstairs to uncork a bottle of wine.

He'd put off grocery shopping again, and without any food in the house, once half a bottle of cheap red had been guzzled, the evening heralded Blotto's arrival. While humming a Cougar Fighters song he'd had in his head all afternoon, Blotto spilled a full glass on the carpet and became intent on sprawling out on the couch. This would have provided a fine setup for lights-out, but Blotto sensed a presence he couldn't fully process at first.

His head throbbed with the velvet unease of dehydrated drunkenness as an alarmed fear came over him: there was someone else in the room.

Synapses firing at maybe a third of their usual speed, this revelation provoked Blotto to have a frenzied flashback to the only other occasion in his life that had prompted such dread in his reptilian brain.

He was in a field near his home, building a maze with his neighbor. The wheat stalks were tall enough that if they crawled around, they could remain a good two inches below the skyline of the natural wonder around them. After two hours of work, they had concocted a vast labyrinth.

Blotto saw through young Luke's eyes. He contemplated the sun high in the sky, remembering with glowing clarity that if he stared straight up, he could discern the curved arc of Earth's distant atmospheric shell. This calmed Blotto, lending him an alignment of deep reserve.

A massive black snake slithered through the stalks and across Luke's bare forearm. Abruptly, bliss was replaced with a blinding terror that slammed every other sense and emotion from his person. Within this mental prison, all that existed was a starfield of indeterminate fright.

And here in Deer Meadow was Luke's snake again, now amplified by the drilling discomfort of Blotto's stupor. Once Luke's heartbeat slowed down, he faded into sleep, but a mystery had begun, one involving an apparition of unknown origin and purpose.

Neither Luke nor Blotto believed in ghosties or goblins, but something was afoot.

Luke awoke a solid hour later than he'd planned and lamented the red wine spill that had set in overnight. By the time he'd cleaned it up and gotten around to sitting in his office chair, it was 10:00 am.

He heard a scratching noise when he went upstairs for coffee, but figured it was the wind knocking tree branches against the side of the house.

15

After having to postpone three days, a grizzly lumber-jack of a man showed up to install the telephone Dalton purchased for Luke. When the technician first saw the contraption, he gave Luke a look like he expected a hidden camera crew and a TV host to pop out and let him in on the prank, but once Luke proved his sincerity, Paul Bunyan went right along and set up the timeworn gizmo.

He had been on a writing jag when the phone was ready to use. If Luke had taken his airplane-hangar headphones off, he would have heard the phone company guy warn that he should be prepared for the Northern Electric Candlestick to boom at foghorn volume when calls started coming in, but Luke never even turned in his chair to acknowledge him.

The technician let himself out.

As Luke cooked breakfast some hours later, the explosion that came from the device inspired one of his hallmark spaz-outs: he splattered eggs and olive oil in all directions. With Luke barely outside the blast radius of Blotto's size-fifteen hangover, this aural napalm was hell as sound.

Luke gripped the part of the telephone he assumed he was supposed to use and was comforted when the device finally stopped screaming at him.

He detected a distant Dalton saying, "You have to wind it three or four times before it works."

Luke surveyed the machine and cranked the only moving part he could find. "Yell-o?" Luke asked.

"You picked up!" Dalton said. "This pleases me."

"I had to."

"Let's get straight to it," Dalton said. "New Dweeb King traffic isn't optimal. You need to do some interviews. Over-the-phoners, no big deal."

"How charmingly exquisite!" Luke said, overdoing it. "This must mean the internet misses me."

"We're down about ten percent."

"That's what we were expecting for this quarter, right?"

"Yeah, but you offering a few choice words about how wonderful the guys are doing without you won't hurt."

"Fine," Luke said, not hesitating.

"What, you're not going to spar with me on this? I usually get ten minutes of grief for every piece of Dweeb information I have to pry out of you."

"I'm having a good day," Luke said, realizing he couldn't pace while tethered to the phone.

"How many pages so far?" Dalton asked.

"I don't know, three? Four, maybe?"

"I ask," Dalton said, "Because I did a test the other day. I took the copy of *Finneran's Rainbow* you forced me to buy last year, which doesn't make any sense at all, by the way, and typed a full page of it on my laptop. Made for almost two computer pages."

"That's not the real name of that book, you know."

"I am to infer, therefore, that today you've written two actual, printable pages."

"I'll probably cut stuff, move elements around…"

"Speed up, daddy-o," Dalton said, "Or you won't meet your deadline. I gotta go. To be continued!"

Dalton ended his phone conversations with Luke using that catch phrase whenever he had the chance, somehow managing to sell its shtick. Luke felt double remorse considering having lied to his agent and friend – he had only written one page that morning.

16

The old man's colloquial directions were surprisingly accurate: Luke easily found his way to Roger's house. What he wasn't expecting was the codger himself, sitting on his deck, looking through a set of binoculars as he monitored the final quarter-mile of Luke's journey.

"You're late," Roger said.

"I got a little turned around."

"You were slow."

Luke set down the twelve pack of beer he'd toted from the store and popped one open. Roger whacked Luke's leg with his cane.

"First of all, you didn't say hello or introduce yourself. Second, you opened a drink before offering one to your host. And third, why the hell did you buy cans? Beer stays colder longer in bottles, dummy!"

Roger grabbed a can himself. He took a long drink, waiting a full five seconds before taking it away from his mouth.

He nodded toward his side yard. "I have a project for you," he said.

Tucked away under a thicket of trees that hadn't yet lost all their leaves was a small porch grotesquely overrun with damp mulch. There wasn't a single spot on the deck that wasn't a good foot deep with the rotting stuff.

"I'll get your shovel," Roger said.

After an hour, Luke's dislike for the janitorial services he was providing peaked. When he came across a dead rat, preserved for who knows how long by the moist juices of this birch tree mush pile, Luke begged Roger for gloves, but he claimed not to have any.

The dumpster in Roger's driveway filled up fast. Luke made the mistake early on of asking whether there were yard waste canisters around, which was answered in the form of a profane diatribe describing what Luke and his New York City hippie recycling buddies should shove up their butts.

At least the two men weren't going thirsty. Luke even began to follow Roger's lead when, upon finishing a beer, he'd toss his empty can right into whatever pile he was processing.

"Why not?" Roger asked.

Luke dropped a scummy collection of leaves and other nauseating things into a wheelbarrow, picking out of it a pack of cigarettes. "I gave up smoking those years ago," Roger said, cackling.

He threw his empty toward Luke and wasted no time cracking another.

"Manual labor is the cure for everything," Roger said, trying to sound as wise as he could, being five beers in. "Best advice I ever got wasn't from no preacher, none of those dumb Bible stories with Noah talkin' to teddy bears or some shit. My grandpappy said when you get pissed off about something, go outside and dig a hole."

"Did you really call him grandpappy?" Luke asked.

Roger gesticulated theatrically, attempting to accent the magnitude of his point. "There isn't a hole, then there's a hole. A beginning and an end. Progress."

A burst of wind shook the leaves on the trees above them. Roger held his beer up.

"Storm's coming."

"There aren't even clouds in the sky," Luke replied.

"See the ring around the sun?"

Luke spotted a circle of faint vapor in the afternoon sky.
"Yeah."

"Sun ring means snow," Roger said. "Probably a foot."

"I'll bet you a beer."

"You're on."

Roger fell asleep halfway through beer number six. Luke
took a long look at him as he snoozed limply in his chair
before placing one last load of leaves into the dumpster. He
wouldn't confess it if Roger ever asked, but this grunt labor
had Luke feeling rejuvenated. He brushed lingering leaf
slime off his shirt and jeans and headed over to the old man.

"You want to go inside?" Luke asked.

Nothing.

Luke sipped the dregs of his warm beer and set the
empty can on the deck. After saying Roger's name aloud six
times to no response, he rustled the guy. Through his vin-
tage Hawaiian shirt, Roger's shoulder felt unusually cold to
the touch, and Luke tapped into a flash of alarm that he had
died while on his watch.

Thankfully, Roger jolted to life. He ticked idly and
reached for his cane. Not saying a word, he entered his
house, closing and locking the front door behind him. Luke
grabbed the last beer for his walk home and made off along
the forest's edge.

It snowed almost two feet that night, shutting down
Deer Meadow for the weekend.

17

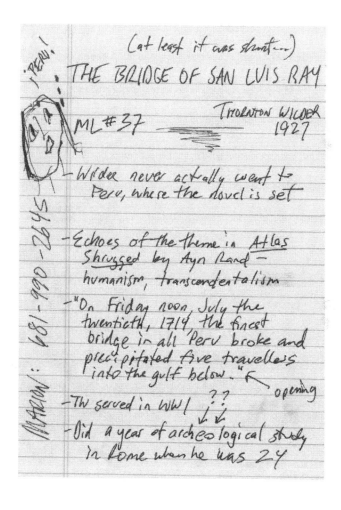

¡PERU!

(at least it was short...)

THE BRIDGE OF SAN LUIS RAY

ML #37 — THORNTON WILDER 1927

MARION: 681-990-2645

- Wilder never actually went to Peru, where the novel is set

- Echoes of the theme in <u>Atlas Shrugged</u> by Ayn Rand — humanism, transcendentalism

- "On Friday noon, July the twentieth, 1714, the finest bridge in all Peru broke and precipitated five travellers into the gulf below." ← opening

- TW served in WW1 ?? ↙↘

- Did a year of archeological study in Rome when he was 24

18

Luke lacked the backcountry ability to brew coffee without the electrical alchemy of his coffee maker, and after two days of power outage, the absence of caffeine in Luke's system left him restless and jumpy. But the massive quantity of snow on his porch was something else. He'd never encountered the otherworldly quiet it brought.

There were no heaters kicking on or computer ding-dongs competing with this calming muteness. Wrapped in not one but two blankets from downstairs, Luke sat near the sliding glass door in his living room – slightly ajar as to hear the snow's aural miracle – and watched the trees in the thicket down the way grow ever heavier with the stuff.

After a meditative morning of this, with an ignoble honk, every device in the cabin crackled back to life. Computers whirred, the microwave beeped, and as printer cartridges realigned themselves and the refrigerator struck up its signature hum, Luke closed the glass door, acquiescing to the siren calls of the modern world.

He made an extra strong pot of joe and plugged in his smartphone that had gone dead, watching it scroll through twenty-five unread messages. It was mostly Dweeb King emails and notes from Ray about football scores at first, but ten items down was an email whose subject was *Wedding*.

Uh-oh, he thought.

What Luke didn't understand until halfway through the message was that the woman looking wistfully into the eyes of a man probably smarter and richer than Luke would ever be was none other than Ashley Hogan, his high school crush.

Luke often thought about utilizing their tumultuous time together as a basis for a romance in a book or script, thinking they had a uniquely shared journey into adulthood, graduating from Pedersen High and traveling in tandem off to college, but he never did. What hung him up was that no matter how he spun or fictionalized the saga, he ended up as the bad guy.

The act of staring at the photo of this bride-to-be popped visions from the past into Luke's head. He'd lost his virginity to her, for starters, and could recall the nervous lead-up to their congress with shining clarity.

Ashley lifting off her bra in his dorm room bed was perhaps *the* definitive moment of Luke's college career, and after he slipped his boxers off in response, lying inches away from her, she took his hand and quietly started to laugh.

It took the edge off. Naked beside her, having barely oblique biological comprehension as to what was about to happen, it was as though Ashley released a pressure valve inside Luke, centering and relaxing him. The sex that afternoon wasn't great, but it didn't make it any less indelibly etched into Luke's brain.

As is the case with most adolescent liaisons like theirs, Luke suspected early on that the two of them would not be together forever. This was where the unmistakably villainous aspect of Luke's story came into the picture, and sitting on his couch, peering at Ashley in miniature on his smartphone, it was still able to prompt a dull thud in Luke's heart facsimile.

Ever the obsessive type, Luke couldn't arrive on the perfect way to end things. A transparent, direct break-up would be a gentlemanly exit strategy, but he lacked the courage to go through with it.

So he didn't.

He decided not to return her calls, not to reach out, not to correspond with Ashley in any way. On a warm spring night, they said their goodbyes as she headed to her dormitory and he went to his, and Luke did not talk to her again. He found a way to avoid her on campus, and answering machine messages didn't add up because when he heard her voice on tape, he'd delete it immediately.

Seeing as they were both from Altoona, there would have to be some creative social calendar gymnastics employed during Thanksgiving and Christmas breaks to keep the two of them from crossing paths, but after two weeks of his cruel freeze-out, Luke got used to the idea.

He'd learn from mutual friends in the months that followed that, beset with grief over Luke's unceremonious betrayal, Ashley ran into the open arms of one of Luke's high school buddies, a man who was balder than he was a decade ago, but identifiable as the co-star in the wedding announcement he was presently reading.

Luke acted like a dick to Ashley Hogan. There was vague merit to the fact he trusted his instincts in the situation, but regardless of how rosy he reconsidered it, his ejection from their couplehood was a bad move.

However, Luke still had a razor-sharp memory of the way Ashley's breasts looked that first time she and Luke were intimate. He'd hold onto that forever.

19

He was deep into a prolonged contemplation as to whether the hair on the backs of his hands was the same color as the hair on his head when a familiar chat beep escaped from Luke's upstairs computer. He grasped his coffee and ascended the stairs.

Luke checked his email and was happy to see a note from Crystal: she had tracked down a copy of *Zuleika Dobson* by Max Beerbohm for him. All this time, a question flashed in the chat program, all but begging Luke to tap into his dormant Dweeb King informational reservoir.

Ray: *Are they ever going to release the original versions of your favorite sci-fi movies on DVD?*

Luke: *Nobody buys DVDs anymore.*

Ray: *I do! GFY.* (Ray's favorite profane texting term: Go Fuck Yourself!)

Luke: *You're a dinosaur, my friend.*

Ray: *If they do come out, I call dibs. When are you back? We need to do a pub quiz.*

Luke: *I don't know. Depends on work.*

Ray: *Tell me this — you probably have a thesaurus open all the time.*

Luke: *I own one, yeah.*

Ray: *How often do you find yourself trying to describe, say, a woman's cans, but not wanting to use that exact word?*

Luke: *I don't know that I've used* cans *in my book yet.*

Ray: *I gotta jet. There's a dollar in it if somebody in your novel says the word* cans.

Ray logged off. As if it were a password or secret code phrase, Luke wrote *cans* on the notepad to his right. After heading into the kitchen for a coffee refill, he heard the ding of the chat program again. Ray must have had another euphemism for female body parts that needed to be shared.

When Luke returned to his computer, there was something off about the program. Whenever he chatted with Luke, Ray's name tag featured a small icon photo of himself, Nicole, and Lori. This current interface was different, blank.

A spinning symbol appeared, indicating someone was typing, and Luke became suddenly afraid.

If he had been able to channel Blotto's long-term memory, he'd have recognized his present state as being identical to how he felt three days back when there was (or wasn't) a presence in the house with him. With eerie, steady slowness, text appeared:

I was someone you knew.

Seeing as it worked fine the last time, Luke pulled the computer's power cord out of the wall. It was likely nothing more than a dopey joke from one of his colleagues – Shelton yanking his chain, perhaps – but Luke felt frayed, dropkicked into a headspace he didn't like. Too on edge to go back to work, Luke went outside and stood on his driveway, desperate to find even a minor distraction to get his mind off the events of the past few minutes.

Mrs. Vicki Packard, Luke's neighbor and lifetime Deer Meadow resident, would tell you she knew Luke was a serial killer the moment she first saw him. She remembered very plainly when, after sorting through junk mail and catalogs brought by her mailman, she stood in the shadows in her second-story living room and watched the young man next door go to the back left corner of his yard with a shovel and begin to dig.

She had wanted to get one of her girlfriends on the telephone, to contact her husband in case this lunatic left the confines of his property and went on a neighborhood killing spree, but she was so curiously perplexed by what was taking place she couldn't move.

There was a bit of snow on the ground, so it was tough going for the man, but after twenty minutes, he'd produced a hole that was maybe two feet deep. Vicki was certain this psychopath was preparing to bury one of the many corpses that had piled up in his house, but after standing over his achievement for a while, he nonchalantly stuck his shovel in the ground and walked back inside.

The rest of that afternoon, whenever Vicki passed her east-facing kitchen window, she'd check to see if the maniac's shallow backyard grave had been filled, but it stayed empty. Her husband told her not to call the cops, that the new tenant wasn't a killer ("He's from New York," he explained), but Vicki kept her eyes peeled all the same.

20

"You really stay in your house all day?" Donna asked. "I'd go crazy."

"Writing is a solitary struggle," Luke said.

"You aren't fooling anybody here with your ten dollar words," Misty replied, pouring a shot for a video poker player down the bar.

"*Struggle* counts as a ten dollar word?"

"Maybe that kind of sass talk is what why you can't get a date," Donna added quietly.

"You two are no help," Luke said, scanning the light Keene's crowd, recognizing Naomi from the post office by her loud laugh.

"Where'd those Romanian ladies head off to?"

"They're vampires, I tell you," Misty said. "They stay inside when the moon is full."

"How can you tell it's a full moon with all these clouds?" Luke asked. "I haven't seen the sky in a week."

"It'll be like this until St. Patrick's Day," Donna said.

She pressed a button that caused her machine to vomit out a steady stream of quarters. "Cash me out $25, Misty," she said.

"You bet."

Donna delicately removed a pack of cigarettes and lit up with the fluidity of a seasoned pro. She half-turned in her seat toward Luke, adjusting her hair ever so slightly.

"Okay. I've had enough," Donna said. "Single people are depressing. Why don't you tell us what sort of lady you'd like to be set up with, and the Cougars of Keene's will see what they can fish out."

Misty spoke in her daytime TV interview voice: "Walk us through your last few ladyfriends."

Luke, acknowledging the humiliating parade he was about to embark upon, took a deep drink. "Well, there was Melissa."

"How many dates?" Misty asked.

"We saw each other for three months."

"Short? Tall?"

"Short."

"Skinny? Busty?"

"Skinny, I suppose."

Donna got in on the action. "And what was she like?"

"She was fun. A little rough around the edges, but we had some good times. She hated wearing shoes. She had a pair of sandals in her backpack for going into a restaurant or whatever, but she preferred being barefoot."

"On the streets of New York City?" Donna asked, appalled.

"Yup."

"This was appealing to you? Maybe you have a little foot thing going."

"I was able to look past it," Luke said, smiling.

"Next!" Donna exclaimed.

"I dated a woman from Texas who was a trip," Luke said. "She was skinny, too. Too skinny. I'm over that. She was very into the pin-up scene."

"A pervert, eh?" Misty said.

"Worse. A hipster."

Misty and Donna sported identical blank stares.

"What you guys would call a New York type."

"We consider *you* a New York type," Misty said.

"Okay, imagine somebody fifty times more New York-y than me."

"Heaven forbid," Donna said.

"So you want us to set you up with a woman who isn't pencil-thin and not a New York type?" Misty asked.

"That's every woman within a hundred miles of here," Donna said.

Luke meekly asked, "Are you sure the Romanians aren't coming back in tonight?"

"They're all working at the casino," Misty said. "Come in on Wednesday to catch them."

"What are they like? Are they nice?" Luke asked.

"They should tip more than they do," Misty said. "Next time you see Marion, tell him Misty wants to know the Romanian word for *tightwad*."

21

The Roger in Luke's dream that night wasn't the gruff geezer he was in real life. In the bleary mists of Luke's wine-soaked mind, Roger appeared as a young man and sat at a desk alongside Luke and his Pedersen High senior classmates, listening to Ms. Linton lecture about *Tobacco Road*.

He was a rugged armed forces type with a farmboy charisma that made him look like he'd stepped out of faded WWII newsreel footage. In fact, the vision played out in black-and-white, with an expressionistic design not dissimilar from Julien Legrand's *Paulette on the Bridge* (CS#348).

As Luke marched up the stairs the next morning, he saw that a foot of snow had fallen overnight on top of the two feet already on his front porch. He wrote through the morning, and around noon, he yielded to the impending chore, optimistically considering the act of shoveling the deck as the equivalent of digging a hole.

Donning as many sweaters and jackets he could find, Luke went out to his shovel's last resting place in the backyard and marched it inside. He barely got his living room sliding door to open, and when he did, Luke lamented how goddamned cold it was. And this precipitation he needed to get rid of was not the powdery fluff ski bunnies swished through in commercials for alpine resort lodges – it was rocky, icy cement.

The snow pack was so impenetrable that Luke felt the shovel threaten to splinter into shards with every motion. Working more discreetly than usual to preserve the integrity of his tool made the task take longer than he hoped, and it was rigorous toil. After spending two hours liberating half the deck from the merciless compacted tundra upon it, a perspiring, irritated Luke called it a day.

Sore from his labors later in the evening, Luke decided to put on a Gunner Hedlund Cornerstone favorite. *Midnight Sun* (CS#214) would appeal both to the frustrated, black heart of his creative side as well as his exhausted mortal coil.

He watched this dark, brooding fable about fears of nuclear annihilation in the 1940s and the argument that God abandoned humankind when man invented fire for twenty minutes before falling into a deep sleep.

Luke's dreams returned to Roger. What did the old man watch when he was home by himself? Did he even own a TV set? Did he have a wife? A kid? Were they alive?

This time they weren't in a Pennsylvania high school, they were in the sharecropping Georgia of *Tobacco Road*, and Roger was driving a Model T past Luke napping under a chinaberry tree.

When Luke awoke, the chill was intense. His lurching cabin heater hardly had a chance to cycle down, constantly trying to keep the place from succumbing to the brutal cold outside. Luke jacked up the thermostat, reasoning that if it was going to be running all day, it might as well be doing so on full blast.

He rummaged through the kitchen for toast or eggs, but
came up short, having not done the grocery shopping he
had needed to do a week ago. Settling for coffee, he turned
out of the kitchen, ready to go to work, only to grumble as
he passed the sliding glass door.

Another foot of snow had fallen overnight, which
meant Luke had to shovel the deck again.

He blamed Roger.

22

As had been the case in his high school days, Luke's
mind wandered while reading *The Catcher in the Rye*. He
couldn't argue against the infamous novel's many literary
assets, but Holden Caulfield's wistful drift through the
graveyard of postwar culture seemed monotonous to him.
As he wrote *Mothers are all slightly insane* on his readily available notepad, Luke broke out of the world of the book,
catching a sound he couldn't discern.

There it came again.

A human was knocking on his door.

Instantly thrown into a panic, Luke surveyed the house
around him and drummed up potential explanations for its
messiness as he tromped downstairs.

Luke may have opened the door hesitantly, but Marion
burst out of the snow into the mudroom with linebacker
intent.

With the blanched distress of a true recluse, Luke stood silently, suspended in shock, until Marion yelled, "Shut the fucking door, man!"

As Luke did so, still not shaking the newness of this impromptu social encounter, Marion embraced him, drawing Luke's body fully to his. After the single longest hug Luke ever staged with a member of his own sex, Marion pulled away and got to the business of taking off his coat and making himself at home.

Marion hung up his winter gear and took off his shoes with meticulous wintertime consideration. Without waiting for any flimsy reason Luke could divine about why it might not be a grand time for a powwow, Marion darted up the stairs.

"Dweeb King. Keep your kitchen cleaner."

"I wasn't expecting company," Luke responded.

Marion didn't waste time examining anything in Luke's living room except the DVDs organized pristinely on his shelves.

"It's great you stopped by," Luke said. "I've wanted to be in touch."

Plainly not sharing his affection for Cornerstone films, Marion turned to Luke, his black eyebrows stressed into a bushy arch. "These are all you have?" he asked.

"Movies? Oh no, I have thousands of them in storage. And packages of new ones arrive every Thursday."

"Those are important. Women want new."

"Women?" Luke asked with a squeak.

Marion put his hand on Luke's shoulder. "Marion will introduce you to beautiful Romanian women," he said. "I promised, didn't I?"

Giving Luke the once-over, he took his chin in his palm. "Tell me. What adjective do you want women to use to describe you? One word."

Luke hated magazine-quiz questions like this. Thinking for a second, he replied, "Fun?"

"Fuck you."

"What? Women like fun guys!"

"Wrong."

"What's your word?"

Marion didn't hesitate, kicking into a smoldering look. "*Lobo.* The wolf."

"You're kidding."

"A fun man will not be fought over by women," he said. "Leave humor and philosophy to men uninterested in making love."

It took all of Luke's willpower not to laugh out loud.

"This will be a long process," Marion said. "What do you have to drink?"

Luke opened his liquor cabinet, revealing two bottles of cheap red wine. Marion was less than pleased.

"First get movies," the Romanian ordered. "Romantic comedies. And have Pinot Grigio American wine ready to serve. A Romanian woman who doesn't drink Pinot Grigio is a witch."

Unconvinced, Luke leered at Marion as he shut the cabinet door. "I can't tell whether you're serious or not."

Marion flashed a fast smile. "See? I am mysterious! I am unpredictable! I am…"

Luke said it for him. "*Lobo.* The wolf. Right."

23

Dalton Ross dressed the part of New York agent extraordinaire. Luke's college pal was not a superficial man (compared to others in his line of business, at least) but he placed great value in the idea that if you wanted to be a mover and a shaker, you had to have the appearance of one. If you needed to be the best-looking agent in a restaurant, *do it*. And should you have a desire to impress the ladies with a nice car, even considering steep Manhattan costs, *do it*.

This last one was where Dalton and Luke never saw eye to eye. Dalton *hated* Luke's car. Every so often, he would bring attention to the fact that because Luke was a sensitive artist type, there were certain personality tics he could get away with that other guys had no chance pulling off.

Case in point: if a mild-mannered agent like Dalton bucked the trend and drove a clunky Cherokee around Manhattan instead of a six-month-old Audi sedan, it wouldn't work. He'd come across as an oddly well-groomed garbage man.

Yet each time Dalton heard Luke kick into the story of why he loved his shitty Jeep so much and how B-Town got her name, he'd witness people in the room unfamiliar with the legend fall victim to Luke's charmingly casual tractor beam.

It went something like this:

By the time the white 1992 Jeep Cherokee had been handed down to Luke, he was a college freshman, and before his first Thanksgiving break, energized by a winning football season, Luke bought what his righteously anti-establishment high school self would have balked: a university bumper sticker.

It was quite a ribbon-cutting ceremony. During a long weekend visiting buddies at a community college in Boston, after getting loaded at a nearby dive, Luke had his pals join him at the vehicle, feeling that affixing said bumper sticker in enemy territory would make his display of honor uncommonly dedicated. To tepid applause, Luke placed his college's bright blue emblem in the lower-right-hand part of the Cherokee's rear window.

The second phase of the B-Town origin story typically began with a new round of drinks, followed by a detailed description of the morning after the bumper sticker commemoration. Luke recounted rooms filled with too many snoring dudes, no open windows, and the hanging haze of nocturnal beer farts.

Once these man-children were awake enough to put one foot in front of another, finding a greasy spoon and a disgustingly caloric meal became prime directive number one, but there was nothing but apartment buildings within walking distance. They needed to pile into Luke's car.

When they arrived at the rattletrap, they saw that it had been vandalized.

A villain in the night had passed the white SUV, appraised its unabashed anti-Boston propaganda sticker, and rejected such a claim, writing in black sharpie underneath the driver's side door handle: "B-Town, Bitch!"

Luke would end his recollection with a reminder that one element of the graffiti had worn away since that fateful day: its comma.

Therefore, B-Town Bitch.

And here she was in Deer Meadow, West Virginia, sounding worse than ever, her undercarriage bellowing like a banshee even on straight roads with slow speed limits. But in a continuing defiance of any vehicular or scientific rationale, the Cherokee ran like a dream. Dalton at one time opined that if you were to lift B-Town's hood, you'd see no engine at all, only a magical, otherworldly power source fueling it along.

The act of driving the car, especially in winter, involved a long list of errant particulars. B-Town's heater hardly ever kicked on. There was a constant rat-a-tat from her rear right wheel, and a heinous whistle blew if the car was driven for more than fifteen minutes at a time. These tics were melodious harmonies to Luke, though to passers-by, B-Town sounded like a tractor that needed a tune-up.

At any rate, as winter went on, when Luke drove into town, he would frequently whiz past fancier, newer vehicles that hadn't been able to successfully maneuver the snowy streets of Deer Meadow without sliding off the road.

If there were a contest for Most Reliable Jalopy in Deer Meadow, B-Town would be a heavy favorite.

24

Luke couldn't shake the exhilaration that had come over him. He had dutifully put in four hours of writing and felt no fatigue or burnout, no misgivings or trepidation. He was worried he'd overused *apparently* in what he'd written but was too pleased with the quantity of material he'd come up with to worry about it (for now). Most outlandish of all, this newfound jubilation made him feel more like getting back to the task at hand than taking his usual extended midday coffee break.

He didn't want to jinx it, but Luke's experiment with The ML100 seemed to be working. Continuing to surround himself with classics in hopes their collective enshrined wisdom would somehow help germinate a vision within him, he regarded his output in the past several days as proof he'd shaken something loose.

He'd never read Walker Percy's *The Moviegoer*, but when he got his copy from the library, Luke remembered a classmate from film school who had raved about it. Toby Chu, a whip-smart avant-garde art brat from Detroit, was the kind of affected aesthete who always gave the impression he was purposefully contrary to any and all pervasive norms and tastes of the age.

On the other side of the aisle from this, as prototypical dingbat undergrads, Luke and his cronies at one point entered a phase in which they went out of their way to be as off-color and distasteful to one another as possible, discovering and often inventing nomenclatures and nicknames that were rude and unseemly, laughing themselves silly at their twisted concoctions.

Luke couldn't recall whether it was Tommy Adams or Keith Burns who got the ball rolling on this inappropriate yet critical topic, but one of them, while doing internet research instead of homework, came across a band named P.F., who were branded as being the single most offensive rock group the world had ever produced. This sort of braggadocio was irresistible, and after a mad rush to Generation Records in Greenwich Village, they encountered the abominable "music" contained on P.F.'s album *Purple Bread.*

It turned out P.F. was short for Piss Flap, and they played atonal death metal sludge. But, oh, the revolting songs. "I'm Glad You're Stuck in Prison" and "Your Dumb Dog" were curling oddball noise anthems, but it was the devilishly mean themes in songs like "Ha Ha, You're Suffering" that left the boys doubled-over, squealing in their enjoyment of the band's tasteless hyperbole.

More background checks on the band and their reprehensible magic ensued, and when it was discovered that the most repellent trio in the world hailed from Toby Chu's hometown, they had to pick his brain.

They went to the editing bay underneath one of the main buildings on campus and found Toby toiling away on whatever existential piece he was working on (for Toby, they weren't *films*, they were *pieces*). Keith did the talking, seeing as Luke and Tommy were prone to guffaw at the mere mention of P.F. song titles.

"You're from Detroit, right?" Keith asked as Toby took off his headphones. "Have you heard of P.F.?"

"P.F.?"

"They're a band," Keith said. "It's short for Piss Flap."

Toby took a moment. "Do they play guitars?"

This cryptic question caused the three visiting morons to exchange a glance before nodding in response.

In one quick motion, before placing the headphones back over his ears, Toby said, "I don't listen to music with guitars in it."

This arty statement became a highfalutin mantra for Luke and his friends, and presently looking out over the snowy expanse of his yard, Luke wondered about Toby. He hadn't considered him or P.F.'s abhorrent racket in years.

And irony of ironies: here he was agreeing with the guy's taste in books.

Luke didn't write later that day, opting to finish *The Moviegoer* on the couch as night fell.

25

A Deer Meadow resident now for a month and a half, Luke had established Wednesday as the one night a week he'd trudge down to Keene's and drink himself stupid. On this particular humpday, after his third gin and tonic, Luke craved conversation. He was *chatty*.

Donna made the mistake of asking how his work was going, which inspired Luke not only to take his sweet time answering her question but to dovetail his lectured response into multiple territories, covering everything from the intricacies of his writing process to the William Faulkner novel he'd been struggling with for two days.

Donna and Misty were regular readers, yet while they logged faint recognition of the famed Southern writer, they harbored no major feelings for him one way or another.

Luke's speech about the author, his titles in The ML100, and his less-than-favorable opinions of them was a numbing, breathless bore, one that drove Keene's patrons to booths outside earshot of the driveling bookish nincompoop who refused to change the subject.

Doing her best to focus on her cigarettes and video poker, Donna vaguely nodded as Luke used phrases like *fucking fruitcake asshole*, waiting for him to turn away before exchanging eye-rolling looks with Misty behind the bar. Luke talked through the evening, even serenading himself about the atypical syntax in *As I Lay Dying* on his way to the men's room.

When it began to snow, Misty instigated an escape plan, telling Luke upon his return from the call of nature that he should get going if he wanted to avoid the brunt of the storm. With quiet elation, the tight-lipped video poker players at the bar returned to their blinking distractions as Luke doofusly attempted to put on his coat.

Misty convinced Luke that cold mountain air would help him come to terms with this author who was causing him such agony, and nearly on the verge of tears, Luke couldn't have agreed with her more. His stature made it appear he had interest in giving Misty a hug before leaving, but she politely waved him along, avoiding physical contact at all costs.

As Luke closed the door behind him, he started right up again with his blathering, walking down the face of the establishment and out into the winter evening. Compensating for Luke's lengthy address, the only sounds made in Keene's for a minute were the pitter-patter of poker machines and the flicking hiss of Donna's newest cigarette.

Luke quickly found himself lost. So vainly immersed in the trickling ooze of his Faulkner-mumbling, he veered off the sidewalk, choosing to stroll through the shadowy depths of the forest in hopes of forging a fresh path home. The way branches played with light, splintering it into a multitude of beguiling shapes and designs, gave his current locale a fantastical aura.

What finally got the guy to shut the fuck up about William Faulkner for the first time in hours was a burst of moonlight on what he slowly discerned was a tombstone. The knowledge that a graveyard was near his cabin made Luke tremble, offering incontrovertible proof this was very much the spiritual home of the ghost who was haunting him.

Luke realized he was completely and utterly alone.

Even at Deer Meadow's most rural fringes, if you were to do a 360-degree survey where you stood, something geographically recognizable would allow you to discern your relative position, but as Luke was attempting this (looking idiotic while walking in slapdash circles), nothing was familiar. Instantly resigned to failure, he was positive he'd die of exposure in this hidden West Virginia graveyard.

Luke then came upon a massive break in the trees that showcased the giant gray Deer Meadow sky. Overtaken by the dynamic change in the nature around him, Luke fell on his back, hitting the packed snow on the ground with a crunchy thud. This gave him a reflective moment to comprehend how drunk he was (*Did I forget to eat dinner again?*, he thought), and his head spun, wondering between cocktail regrets about the composition of the vast universe that existed beyond the storm streaming above him.

He turned his head and saw an alien relic sticking out of the ground like a Mayan totem. Was this a Cro-Magnon weapon of some sort? Had he discovered a new civilization? Ah, no: this was the flag for the fourteenth hole of the Deer Meadow golf course. Luke made his way back onto his feet and used the curve of the snowy fairways to steer himself home.

His couch was damp for three days after this, seeing as Luke slept on it without bothering to take off his coat or boots.

26

After avoiding it for longer than any decent adult should, Luke admitted to himself that there wasn't a clear path from his bed to the coffee maker. Piles of dirty clothes and garbage of curious varieties had accumulated in unkempt swatches on the floor.

It was time to dig out.

Two hours of uninterrupted domestic misery later, all evidence of empty wine bottles and instant burrito wrappers were whisked into trash bags, and Luke kicked on the dishwasher, prompting its loud purr. Clothes were picked up, notepads were collected and slated for input into the computer, and DVDs were carefully recataloged.

Downstairs was an even more chaotic snow bum mess. The load of laundry he started a week ago had re-dried in the washer and now needed a second cycle. Dirt and melted snow puddles littered the mudroom floor, and an array of loose change joined pieces of lint that had taken up shop atop the dryer.

As Luke looked down the hallway, he saw a line of clothes littering it from the front door to the bathroom, which was in shambles. The bedroom was nominal in terms of human shrapnel, which surprised Luke until he remembered he'd slept on the living room couch all week.

Luke peeked at his reflection in the small mirror at the side of the office, acknowledging that he was still only wearing the boxer shorts he'd slept in. He stared at himself for a while.

He was the kind of guy who was never terribly well manicured when it came to shaving or hair-combing, but his beard was bushier than normal, and the hair on his head was a train wreck. Moving closer to the mirror, Luke appraised his bare torso, realizing there was less to him than usual.

Not interested in pondering the cause or meaning of this freshly recognized body transformation, he turned to his writing desk, in every way the workplace of a crazy person. Notes were strewn all about, and a foot-tall mountain of wadded idea rejects was ingloriously piled near the door.

Luke began compiling the seemingly patternless collection of papers on display. He arranged the notes by topic and content and soon found himself thrilled by what they were assembling to become. He may have had bags under his eyes, and his bitter breath may have reeked from the coffee he was drinking too much of, but Luke's bizarre outlining process was focusing his narrative sharply.

Something had snapped, been reduced to its bare bones. There was an ocean of jottings that still required processing, but before getting to them, Luke contemplated the sorcery at his fingertips. At this lunatic's desk, progress was being made.

It was *working*.

27

MIDNIGHT'S CHILDREN

ML# 90   SALMAN RUSHDIE
                                  1980

"This, then, was the
beginning of my first exile.
(There will be a second,
and a third.)" ← ironic,
                    considering SK
                    ↑ Satanic Verses

— considered a very
«Indian» book.
            — magical/
                realism

Dense but approachable ↙
his best?   how does he
                       keep this from
                       going too far?

← good none

DAYLIN ←

28

Getting to the Charleston airport from Deer Meadow
was an ordeal that involved distilling awful directions from
locals who knew less than they claimed about their area's
general geography and a threatening convolution of winding
country roads, but once Luke parked B-Town at the terminal and boarded his flight to Gotham, all travails of his
rough journey fell away.

On the two-hour flight, he sipped martinis, made it
through an episode of *Paris Underground* (CS#402) on his
laptop, read the first thirty pages of *Catch-22*, and scarfed
down a cranberry-chicken sandwich that was so good he
flirted with the flight attendant to bogart a second.

In no time, Luke gave Scott, Dalton's running back of a
driver, a high-five, and watched the turnpike become Manhattan street grids. Luke still recognized the intersections
and stores they passed, even recalling why Scott avoided
certain blocks and neighborhoods, but by the time he arrived at Dalton's Tribeca brownstone, he felt like a tourist.

"You look terrible," Dalton said. "I love it."

Dalton embraced Luke warmly and led him through the
simply-furnished domicile to his office. Luke dropped his
duffel bag on the floor and collapsed into the room's enormous leather couch.

Dalton gnawed off a piece of nut-berry energy bar.
"What can I tell the publisher? Got a title yet?"

"Nope."

"A tagline, maybe?"

"Don't have one."

Luke could tell by Dalton's loud chewing that his agent wasn't happy with these answers. Aiming to inspire some confidence, Luke added, "But things are really coming together."

Dalton felt a trout on the line. "You've been holding out on me," he said. "Go!"

Luke sat upright on the bulky sofa and laid it all out, recounting how much writing he was churning out, channeling a zeal for his process Dalton was sincerely surprised by. It was Luke's turn to be perplexed when Dalton reacted with excited positivity to his ML100 project and how it was fueling his creative locomotion.

"Is *Visitor From the Outer Banks* on the list?" Dalton asked.

"Not much science-fiction there."

"That's a shame."

Luke finished outlining what the coming weeks would bring and vowed he'd have a wealth of material to share with the publisher before Christmas.

Pointing at Luke, Dalton yelled with jokey ardor, "Don't you fuck with me, Luke Sullivan!"

"Scout's honor," Luke said.

"Do me a quick favor, though" Dalton added. "You'd lower my blood pressure significantly if you told me *what the fuck your book is about.*"

"Can't we go have a drink or something first?"

Dalton got out of his chair and sat on his desk. "We'll do plenty of that tomorrow. Give me a hint. Sell me."

Luke looked up into space, taking his time. "It's about a woman," he said slowly, "who goes crazy."

"Is there romance?" Dalton asked. "Tell me there's romance."

"There is. A lot."

"And at least one person dies. Maybe the boyfriend or the husband – that's very hot right now."

Luke took his time getting up out of the couch and stood near Dalton confidently. "I'll say this. The movie version will absolutely be R-rated. Bloody as hell. Tons of nudity."

Dalton gave Luke an exaggerated kiss on the forehead and insisted it was time for dinner.

29

The Oklahoma game was on at 1:00 pm, which meant the first beers of the day would be opened over breakfast. As Dalton and Luke walked from the diner on Hudson Street they both loved to a Sooner-friendly bar four blocks away, Luke realized this college football Saturday was the first full day off he'd had in months.

Friendly outings with Dalton were particularly relaxing because he was the sort of guy who left his work entirely at the office. During billable hours, Dalton was no-nonsense all the way, but the minute quitting time arrived, the designer clothes flew off and the flip-flops came on. Luke was the antithesis of this, a writer always working at some facet of his method, but today was all play and no work, which was fine by both of them.

They got to Golsen's an hour early to lock down the best table in the place, one with easy access to dartboards and pole position TV exposure. The beer flowed, and after an hour spent covering a wide cross-section of topics, Dalton and Luke made a bet that whoever lost the next game of darts would pay for lunch.

The appearance of Phil and T.J., two longtime pals of Dalton's from OK, instigated another turn in the day. There were general greetings, orders of Buffalo wings, and hoarse yelling whenever the Crimson and Cream scored, and before they knew it, the Sooners were ahead by thirty going into the second half.

Dalton decided their Oklahoma contingent – Luke was one of them by proxy, they'd drunkenly insist –shouldn't waste precious drinking hours watching such a blowout, so they settled their surprisingly manageable bill and searched for a quieter watering hole, maybe one with a view.

Luke had never been to Oklahoma. Phil, a slight and acerbically charming graphic designer, described Tulsa as the most humid place in the lower forty-eight, declaring that the act of simply walking outside in August heat was akin to sixteen hair dryers blowing at your face and armpits on full blast. Phil was also confident the water supply in the suburb he lived in for two decades was to blame for the steadily increasing girth and receding hairline he was dealing with as an adult.

T.J., as Luke discovered at the third bar they limped to, might have been congenial and soft-spoken while sober, but after throwing back a few, the accent he had to have spent deliberate energy subduing in his business life was back in roaring fury. By 4:00 pm, he was *slaying* Luke with bawdy Osage County phraseology. Luke would have sat there the rest of the day listening to these Southerners banter, but Phil had a better idea. It was time to hit the town.

This is where the wheels fell off the wagon for Luke.

The morning beer had refreshingly trickled down his gullet, and the gin and tonics the men turned to in the afternoon were decidedly better than the ones Misty made back in Deer Meadow, but Luke hadn't been in the mood for the finger foods the day had presented to him, which opened the door to a familiar character.

Dalton, Phil, and T.J. may have entered their first club of the evening with Luke, but when they left, they did so with Blotto as their fourth.

As it so often happened, after barreling through a trio of high-profile nightspots, Dalton convinced the group they needed to settle into an easy evening finale, so they ended up at his favorite greasy spoon. Being the bubbly chatterers they were, it didn't take long for a quartet of co-eds to join them in their booth, sipping boozy drinks Phil loudly insisted would go on his tab.

What started as basic flirtation turned sour on a dime when Phil demanded to know how old the girls thought he and his friends were. Dalton did everything in his power to divert this conversation from its inevitable stinging ending, but Phil wouldn't let it go.

That was when Blotto got the hiccups.

Since childhood, a case of the hiccups was anathema to Luke. He'd get them once, maybe twice a year, and they were no fleeting minor afflictions. When they arrived, they took over Luke's person with violent, ungovernable ferocity, causing physical pain as well as acute psychological distress.

He'd gone to the hospital for them twice in adolescence, and those visits inspired no illuminating diagnosis about how his esophageal holocausts could be restrained or even blunted.

When Luke got the hiccups, it was *bad*.

There was a certain way Luke could drink a glass of water that involved craning his head back, pinching his nose, and swigging in big gulps instead of dainty sips that sometimes ushered his episodes to closure, but it wasn't working. Blotto's weird-ass behavior was not helping the men appeal to the ladies at the table, and Dalton determined the only way to keep them all content was to send Blotto back to his brownstone.

Dalton made Blotto repeat the last part of his instructions five times: he had to leave the front door open. Dalton had an access code for the main door of his building, but never having gotten around to making a spare key, it was crucial for both Blotto and the good times boys that his guest remember this part of the arrangement.

Blotto agreed, and Dalton shoved him into a cab on 55th Street, giving the driver a twenty.

Luke woke up at 6:00 am, and while he could recognize with strong confidence he had had too much the night before, he was able to get himself out of bed and hit the showers at Dalton's place after only a short bout of unease. Freshened up and ready for the day, he ventured into the main rooms of the house.

No one was around. No Phil or T.J. slumped on the couch, no Dalton in a state of disarray in his room. Luke was alone.

Initially upset that the guys had kicked into party day two without waking him, he dug into his bag and unearthed his smartphone, which had been asleep for days. He plugged it in, and as soon as that home screen popped on, he saw he had thirty-five missed calls since 3:30 am.

Nervously, Luke checked his messages. He only needed to listen to one to know he needed to get Dalton on the line immediately.

A haggard voice answered. Luke meekly said, "I am *so* sorry."

"I'll be there in ten minutes."

It turned out Dalton had tried for an hour to wake Luke up by knocking on his front door, then wandered around Tribeca all night, opting not to go all the way back to Long Island with T.J. and Phil.

Not many words were exchanged between Dalton and Luke once the owner of the house Luke had slept so soundly in made his belated return. Dalton gave him a quick hug and said while exchanging his rumpled club gear for a Dallas Cowboys t-shirt and shorts, "This is it. Your time. The one you get."

What Dalton never knew – and Luke would never be able to recall – was that on his way to Tribeca that night, Blotto got out of the cab early, walked in the wrong direction for nearly twenty blocks, and barfed in a shrub in front of a quiet co-op on 58th Street.

Blotto, full on idle.

30

While looking at a photograph of the Powells magnetized to his refrigerator, Luke realized he didn't know exactly what his duties were as godfather. He had established a gentleman's agreement with Ray and Nicole years ago when they'd offered Luke the title (with Nicole imploring that the two men keep themselves from quoting the bloody gangster epic during the ceremony), but Luke never bothered to determine what the hell – *Sorry, Jesus*, he thought – was expected of him in the job.

He asked about any nearby Methodist churches while at Keene's the next Wednesday, and Misty knew a guy. Arrangements were made, and on a bright Friday morning, Luke drove to Trinity Methodist Church five miles south of town. He walked into the unobtrusive place, and a smiling man who reminded Luke of a friendly accountant shook his hand firmly.

Pastor David Mangi took Luke into his clean, austere office and talked baseball. Dave coached both spring and summer league teams and was disappointed he had to wait through winter until opening day was next upon them.

They spoke about the many trophies in the room and toured the enlarged photos and banners that graced each wall. After slapping his knee with confidence knowing his wife would recognize Luke from TV, Dave clasped his hands together and gave Luke the look he'd been dreading since he arrived.

"So you're a godfather," Dave said. "That's a very important job."

"I have no idea what I should be doing."

"This young couple picked you to be their child's spiritual representative. It's a testament to your personal value."

Luke wasn't sure how to follow this.

"Do they both attend weekly services, or is it more one than the other?

"Well, Ray *goes* to church all the time, and Nicole will…"

As though he was reading his mind, Dave finished for him, "…go for Christmas and Easter."

Dave kept on as though he'd recited this speech three times already that day.

"It happens all the time with new parents," he said. "There are certain compromises that can be made on the subject, but it boils down to the fact that sometimes one parent cares very deeply about it and the other does not. To one dear friend of yours, you've made an eternal pact witnessed by your community, your church, and God. To the other, you've placated a spouse by performing rehearsed dialogue while dressed in your Sunday finest."

"You make it sound like I've committed a crime," Luke said.

Dave tapped his fingers next to a photograph of what must have been his wife and kids.

"I assume you are not a churchgoer," he said, not exactly prompting a response. "This is what I tell non-religious folks on this one. If you nobly act as spiritual steward to this kid, and it turns out at the end of your life that there never was a man upstairs, you will have spent your days giving a child more love and attention than he or she would have received if you were just another friend of the family. Good on you."

"If there *is* somebody up there, and I'm sure that's the case, if you're a good godfather, it will look great on your resumé when you reach the pearly gates."

Still unconvinced, Luke asked, "But as far as…?"

"Did these parents come to you with specific requests about what the godfather of their child is supposed to do?"

"No."

"Do you think if you weren't holding up your end of the bargain, your friends would let you know?"

Luke considered this for a moment, not needing to answer the pastor out loud.

Dave told Luke to give Misty his best as they said their goodbyes outside the church. The pastor's last words to him weren't of any significant religious import – Dave insisted Luke try Keene's famous winter chili next time he was there.

31

Marion assured Luke there was no decent place within a hundred miles of Deer Meadow to buy clothing for his debut on the Romanian dating scene, but Marion had housemate Luke's size and was happy to share. It took Luke's Romanian pal ten minutes to dash over to the cabin, and his unbearable fashion show began.

Luke timidly went to the corner of his bedroom to change into the first trousers Marion recommended, so as not to be up close and personal with the Romanian in his varying states of undress, but Marion didn't want to miss anything.

Once Luke let his baggy blue jeans fall to the floor, Marion was quick to point to Luke's torn boxer shorts. "Women don't like that," he said.

The clothes were going to be tight. Even considering his recent weight loss, Luke was a little broader than Marion's buddy, and where Luke preferred looser apparel, Deer Meadow Romanians liked their skinny jeans *snug*. After addressing the inevitable bunching that came with this, Marion evaluated Luke's new threads and decided it all depended on finding the perfect shirt.

Everything was black. Materials and textures varied slightly from garment to garment, but no shirt he tried on registered a shade brighter than midnight dark. Three attempts in, Luke gazed at himself in his bathroom mirror with tentative self-confidence. The pants weren't right, but from the waist up, he was almost presentable.

"What do you think?"

Spinning Luke slowly, Marion said, "She can see your body. She'll love it."

Marion made a valiant attempt to tame the insane explosion of Luke's hair but aborted that mission after only a few moments. The Romanian sneakily doused Luke with some of his cologne and smiled at his creation.

"And now, women," he said.

Luke couldn't believe how many people lived in the place. Marion led him into the entry room of an apartment near the casino outside town, and there were at least twenty pairs of shoes strewn about.

Romanian voices hummed behind closed doors.

Marion said, "She won't talk to you. But that's okay."

"What?"

"She only listens." Marion picked a piece of lint off of Luke's borrowed shirt. "She doesn't speak English yet, but she will."

Luke held his breath as they entered the kitchen, which was overlit with fluorescence. Marion's misshapen girlfriend Kristina took a long drag from an unfiltered cigarette and approached Luke briskly.

"You bring movies?" she demanded.

Luke had originally intended to offer the girls a bouquet of flowers, but Marion insisted the girls were bound to respond more favorably to movies than nature. The box of review discs from Dweeb King had arrived a few days earlier, and Luke handed Kristina the titles Marion selected for them. The ogress perused them eagerly.

Marion ushered a dazed Luke toward the oven, and the bachelor paused in surprise. A woman with long black hair turned from something exotic-smelling on the range and looked at him – well, *toward* him – keeping her head at an adorable tilt as she waved hello. Luke felt compelled to kiss her hand.

Her name was Anya.

There was not a lot of dinner conversation. Salad tongs clanged, and Luke heard hushed Romanian asides, but for the most part, it was the quietest double date he had ever experienced.

Luke utilized a pattern of staring intently at his food, taking a few bites, then discreetly turning Anya's way, lingering on her face for as long as he could without prompting her to look back at him. During the soup course, he surveyed a sea of freckles that was more prevalent on her right cheek than her left.

Marion and Kristina were all business with the food in front of them. This was less a formal dinner than it was feeding time at the trough, an opportunity for them to amass nutrition as rapidly as possible. The minute the last morsel of foodstuff was thrust into Marion's mouth, he crashed his utensils onto his plate and took a cigarette out of his shirt pocket, lighting it with a dart.

Noticing Luke peering his way, Marion tapped Anya on the shoulder, whispering in Romanian. Luke hoped to get some form of definition from Marion as to what had taken place, but all he got was a thumbs-up.

They didn't stay long. Kristina and Anya took the DVDs into the living room, and without any goodbyes, Marion pushed Luke toward the front door.

Putting on his coat, Luke asked Marion quietly, "What did you ask her?"

"Whether she thought you looked better on TV or as a real person."

"And?"

The Romanian squeezed Luke's cheeks. "Marion's matchmaking is good, no?"

32

He was half a bottle of wine in, and therefore unable to produce enough manual dexterity to get a fire going. In search of a cozy resting place, with fumbling, drunken clumsiness, Luke stripped to his underwear without bothering to close any drapes (*West Virginia, you're welcome!*, he thought), grabbed the remaining bottle and his too-full glass, and headed downstairs.

As he swigged Cabernet half-naked in his room, Luke realized his specter was back. It had been a while since it last stopped by, and the liquid courage in Luke's hand gave him a gabby desire to interact with it. Deciding to speak in a louder voice than normal in hopes of scaring the demon back to hell, Luke monologued.

"Make as many creepy sounds as you want. I ain't taking SHIT from you, you piece of shit!"

(swig)

"You've seen it, you know? You were present at your own death. Did you go right through to the other side, man, or did you have to wait around? Does somebody tell you how it was all supposed to work? Do you ever get hungry? Do ghosts pee?"

(pause)

"I know your line of work must be super tough, but you know what? I put in six straight hours today. I got a lot done. Well, maybe it wasn't six straight hours. Seeing as you can probably walk through walls and time travel and all that shit, you know everything. Fuck you."

(swig)

"I don't need to explain anything to you! You're sitting there, invisible, reading my mind. What number am I thinking of, you piece of shit? HA! I'm not thinking of a number. I'm thinking of a bumblebee. PSYCH! I'm not even thinking about that!"

(pause)

"Here's a question for you, alien overlord or whatever

you are. If you see the ghost of W. Somerset Maugham around, will you punch him in the nuts for me? I read that goddamned bullshit book of his, and it was long and stupid and BORING."

(swig)

"So send your fucking message! Should I go out and buy an Ouija Board to make it easier for you? Wait, you know what? Screw that! You want to haunt me? Do your job, ghost!"

(empty bottle falls to the floor)

"I don't want to look at you, though. No offense. You're scary as shit already, and if you have some sort of fucked-up face, I don't want to know about it. You're mean, you know that? Haunting people is mean. And do you haunt me when I'm in the shower? That is rude. You're a dick, perv."

(pause)

"Thanks for the company."

Luke jolted to life at 4:00 am, in shock from the cold. He'd fallen asleep with the light on, lying on top of the covers on his bed. He groaned with wine-haze numbness as he switched off his clock's upcoming alarm. He woke up three hours late and almost tripped on the empty wine bottle upon getting out of bed.

After an abortive few hours trying to write, Luke put on his galoshes and spent ten minutes digging a hole out back, hoping to stir the muse, but the act only made him interested in taking a long afternoon nap, which he did.

33

Of the many theories that came rushing to his mind the afternoon the noises started, the one that scared Luke the most was that the scratching coming from outside had been there since he moved in and he hadn't detected it until that very moment. Defaulting to daydreams of hungry bears or flocks of rabid woodpeckers on the attack, Luke attempted to logically assess the issue at hand.

He first considered what the scraping *couldn't* be. The coffee maker, the toaster, the water heater – he isolated each of these sounds and felt confident the clamor was not originating in any of the house's appliances. Luke turned faucets on and off, tested light fixtures, and paid extra attention to the reliably rattling heater, but it and everything else checked out.

Luke put on his boots, trod past the partially snowed-over dug holes in his yard, and faced the exterior side of the wall in question. He sniffed around for any tracks in the snow that might confirm that a mountain lion or a Yeti had been attempting to claw into the house, but he saw nothing out of the ordinary.

Too bad he didn't know Mrs. Packard next door was watching him through her dining room window – she'd have been able to tell him that no animals had been in the area, at least not for the last half hour or so.

After returning inside and setting up another pot of coffee, Luke stood in the center of the living room and listened for a while, making sure whatever had possessed that area of the house was now gone. On his way downstairs, Luke chalked the whole business up to a hangover remnant posing as a tap-tapping intruder.

Crisis averted.

The sounds reappeared ten minutes into Luke's writing session. He made one more trip outside (to Mrs. Packard's great thrill), but the only evidence of snow monster invasion were the boot prints he made when he had been out there earlier. When the sounds came back a third time, Luke knew he needed to stage an intervention.

Instead of calling somebody from the pound or searching for Deer Meadow's handiest bug man online, Luke thought he'd save a little coin by getting Roger's advice on the matter. Surely he would know what kind of tell-tale heart had beset itself into Luke's rental.

He bought a six pack of beer and swung by the old man's house, feigning a surprise neighborly visit. Roger was happy enough to see that Luke had finally wised up and chosen bottles, but was less responsive to his requests for aid.

"I need you listen to something strange," Luke said.

"Why? To what?"

"That's just it. I'm not sure."

"Will you pick up more beer on the way?"

"Yeah, sure."

Still cheaper than calling an exterminator, he thought.

Roger farted with a muted honk on his way up the stairs. Just as he finished his second beer, the scratching re-appeared. Luke looked to Roger for confirmation that this noise wasn't coming from inside his head.

Roger nodded knowingly. "Nothing to be worried about."

He staggered over to the wall and pounded it with his fist. "SHUT UP, YOU LITTLE FUCKERS!"

The noise stopped.

"This time of year," Roger began, "critters either go into the woods and stay there through spring, or they find a nice little nook where they can stay warm until the snow melts. Some Deer Meadow chipmunks have found a way into your house."

The old man took great pleasure in seeing Luke's face turn white.

"Don't get worked up," Roger added. "It's not like they're going to be watching TV with you or anything. They've dug into the insulation in the wall. It isn't a bad set-up. They eat all sorts of bugs."

"Chipmunks don't eat bugs!" Luke said nervously. "They gather acorns and shit!"

"Give it a few days, and the scratching will stop," Roger said. "You'll be fine until summer."

"What happens then?"

"That's when the babies are born."

On the ride back, Roger repeatedly assured Luke that once the rodents had settled in, they'd be quiet, and he would no longer be living in the place when spring converted the insulation in his walls into chipmunk nurseries.

After returning home, Luke suffered visions of waves of chipmunk babies being conceived (gross) then born (even worse) prompting the walls of the place to explode with varmint undesirables, but as it turned out, Roger was right: two days later, the scratching stopped.

34

(at least he finishes his sentences in this one.)

LIGHT IN AUGUST,
ML #54   William Faulkner
                              1932

- heavy drinker — liked a
  mint julip in a metal glass
- would celebrate finishing a novel
  by going on a bender

- I bet hearing someone read it
  aloud makes it better

- VGH ——

        gave up on page 365

        Seriously, screw this guy.

My favorites on the list: frontrunner.

35

Luke's heart sank when Marion told him Anya wanted Keene's to be the site of their first official date. Deer Meadow had zero other dining options, he supposed, but the idea of Donna, Misty, and passerby Romanians peeking into what was bound to be a tumultuous chaperone-free evening had danger written all over it.

He brought flowers this time, hoping a display of American welcome would counter his dorkier attributes. When Marion saw Luke approach Anya's apartment with them, he didn't even bother signaling disapproval, instead taking them out of Luke's hand and throwing them to the side of the entryway, out of sight.

Luke was not asked inside this time. Marion held the front door halfway closed and, restricting Luke from watching their exchange, spoke with Anya feverishly in their native tongue. Their discussion ended with Anya pleading for something and Marion refusing to engage with her.

"ONLY ENGLISH!"

Swimming in the suit he knew he had become too small for, Luke found a latent thrill in seeing that Anya looked equally askew. Humbly clad in what seemed like borrowed clothes, she clenched a shiny purse and peered at her suitor.

As Marion left the young lovers to themselves, Luke wasn't sure if it was simply the advent of a woman giving him the time of day or Anya herself entrancing him, but warmth rose in his chest as they clumsily acknowledged each other.

When he opened the front door to Keene's, it was as though they entered a sitcom version of Deer Meadow. Not only were the usual suspects in attendance, but Luke even caught a glimpse of Pastor Mangi in a corner booth with his family, waving at them.

The gang was all here.

Doing what he could to ignore these familiar presences, Luke was every bit the gentleman as he and Anya nestled into one of the quieter booths in the restaurant. After ten seconds of silence, Luke was blindsided by the fact he couldn't strike up a conversation. He considered tackling yes/no questions Anya might giggle at in response, but he didn't want to take the risk of putting her on the spot.

Misty appeared, sporting an amplified grin. "What are we drinking?"

Luke asked Anya, "Would you like a glass of wine?"

"Shoot, honey," Misty sassed. "You're on a date! Order the most expensive cocktail on the menu!"

"Which is what, exactly?" Luke asked.

"Probably a double Jaeger shot with a tequila chaser."

Luke jokingly looked to Anya. "Please don't order that."

He and Misty chuckled, but this off-hand rapport caused Luke's date to zip instantly into deer-in-headlights alarm, wondering what these Americans were saying about her that was so funny. She saw Marion and the Kristina monster enter the establishment. Anya waved them over vigorously. Marion gave Misty a high-five and winked at Luke before Anya tugged him down to whisper in his ear.

"Only English," Marion calmly said. "We all must learn the language of this beautiful country. Right, stud?"

Misty followed Marion and Kristina around the bar, saying to Luke, "I'll give you guys a minute."

Fumbling with his fork, Luke expected Anya to send him an internationally recognizable signal that the date was over, but she returned to calm quickly, giving Luke the same glued-on smile she'd sported since he picked her up.

They fiddled with napkins and ketchup bottles between short, polite exchanges of eye contact, but when Misty got waylaid by a skiing buddy of hers and ten minutes of dusty speechlessness passed at their table, Luke became ready to establish a time of death on the date. Confident Anya felt the same way, he nodded toward the door.

She was more enthusiastic about this than she'd been about anything that night.

Snow started to fall during the drive from Keene's to Anya's apartment. When B-Town pulled into her building's parking lot, Luke felt the pregnant hesitation that comes at the end of most first dates. The two of them sat there, eyes straight ahead, silent. Thirty seconds later, Anya opened her door and ran inside.

Aware he hadn't offered to escort her in, Luke jarred open his door and stood on his seat, his head rising over the layer of snow on B-Town's roof. "I'm sorry!" he yelled.

Luke put his seat belt back on, not seeing Anya's front door open again. She surprised him, appearing outside his driver's side window. With a shy motion, she pointed into B-Town's back seat, where Luke's review DVDs sat in a pile.

Breathing hastily in the cold, Anya gave him three rapid waves gesturing him to follow her, and jogged back up the pathway. Luke parked B-Town, picked up the discs, and went inside.

What happened next wouldn't have set anyone's nighties on fire, but without any of her roommates bothering them, the remainder of their night was relaxed and genial. Anya uncorked a bottle of Pinot Grigio and made a happy cheep when she saw the cover of a ridiculous romantic comedy involving a divorcee and a baby kitten in Luke's stash.

And Anya didn't sit at the opposite end of the couch when it was movie time. Luke wasn't vigilantly trying to put the moves on her – the fact they were still *on* this date was success enough – but they sat relatively close through the entire abominable film in content peace.

Luke wondered what Anya and her friends would gossip about when he left. He also made out a slight hint of flowery perfume in the air, and every time she raised her glass of wine, he saw the outline of a thin brassiere resting on her shoulder.

36

He passed a man putting snow chains on a brand new SUV on the way to the grocery store, patted B-Town's dashboard with pride, and considered with rhapsody the car's eccentricities while waiting at a stop light.

Her passenger-side rear window that only rolled up part of the way. Her hatchback that needed the assistance of a Gandalf-worthy walking stick to stay propped open. The roaring, mangled gnarl whenever Luke shifted gears. The shattered glass and mutilated fiberglass of her external injuries over the years.

To her driver, this car was a broken but iridescent gem. Jolting Luke out of this was an ear-piercing *thump-thump-thump*. He drove through the intersection for a block or two, hoping the car had run over a piece of garbage that'd spit itself out of the vehicle's undercarriage somehow, but the sound remained.

Damning his decision not to put his smartphone in his pocket upon leaving the house, he parked B-Town on the side of the road, trudged a mile home in the snow, and called Keene's in hopes of catching Donna, whose husband was the town's most trusted mechanic.

Donna arranged to get Luke in right away, so he drove the atrociously loud car to Mr. Evans' small garage, and was relieved to see Donna, who had decided to meet him there. She shook hands throughout the office, and saved up a full kiss for the ball and chain, a Native American gentleman named Avery who sported long gray hair and a thin beard.

Luke was certain his video poker expert pal was going to get him a helluva deal. They'd probably connect a hose, remove a part, charge him fifty bucks for labor, and send him on his merry way. Again B-Town would defy the odds and keep on truckin'.

"Have you been monkeying with the odometer?" Avery asked.

"Nope."

"400,000 miles is pretty good for a Jeep this old."

"The tip of the iceberg, I hope."

The man unlatched the open hood and let it crash. "That sound was a belt that fell out of whack," he said. "I put it back on, but don't expect much. My advice is to ride her until she dies."

"How long do you think she has?"

"A day, a month, maybe longer. I'm surprised you can even get it to start."

Luke drove B-Town to the cabin, the car displaying the blend of wheezes and sputters she'd been making for years now. From then on, Luke always took a quick moment before starting the vehicle, bracing himself that any day could be B-Town's last.

37

"Garbage," cried Misty, slamming the paperback on the counter.

Temporarily upgraded from his status as casual Keene's patron, Misty had invited Luke to her house for a barbecue, and he was late. He barely had a chance to put the beer he had been ordered to bring into her icebox when Misty laid into him about the novel he suggested she read. Her first expressive phrase on the topic, in fact, involved the extra large bag of dicks Luke could suck before recommending any more titles for her.

"I am a smart woman!" Misty exclaimed as she forced a plastic spigot into a box of wine. "And I have no idea what that fucking book was about."

"It's not necessarily *about* anything, it's…"

Cutting off her guest, and now armed with a plastic cup of box Chardonnay, Misty spoke with a concerned tone.

"You're not," she said, pointing to the paperback like it

was a murder weapon, "writing a book like *that*, are you?" Donna looked at the novel's cover and shook her head. "I've never heard of it."

"It was not fun to read," she insisted. "Case closed." Unable to resist joining Misty, Luke poured himself a cup of box wine and sealed his fate with a question he thought would inspire jokey lightness.

"What, and every book in the world needs to be fun?" Misty took a step toward Luke and booed him loudly. This prompted them both to laugh, and after Misty demanded her husband throw the paperback onto the barbecue coals (before realizing how awful those burned pages would make the meat taste), the shindig reset itself.

Later they both returned to the Chardonnay box at the same time. "Didn't mean to be so harsh earlier," she said. "Only trying to keep it real."

Ever the bartender, Misty placed Luke's glass under the spigot. "We want our dweeb to become rich and famous so we can all stay at his beach house," she added. "But we'll be a million miles away if you write junk like that."

38

Luke deemed Monday a Cornerstone night, after being inspired by a video sent to him from a pal from the CS forum in which director Marcus Maston got access to what Luke's online evil twin Gus Van Cant called The Throne Room, a small chamber in Cornerstone's office where they kept their precious inventory.

After writing straight through the afternoon (and scrolling through the Maston video three more times), Luke went out and bought ingredients to make a proper supper, a step up from the elementary chicken breast with salt and pepper he'd become so used to fixing for himself. As dusk settled in, he lit a candle and took arty delight in considering what film he was going to revisit.

The bottle of wine he'd also purchased at the store was valued at just over seven American dollars, so compared to his usual rotgut, it was the nectar of the gods. He poured a glass, recited CS' mission statement – "…an evolving collection of diverse masterworks from around the globe, presents…" – and approached the shelf.

Luke knew he wasn't in the mood for a heavy work like the WWI documentary *Forged Trenches* (CS#184), but he pulled out the DVD's booklet essay anyway, scanning for Kevin Turney's name in the Production Credits section, glowing with glee upon finding it right where it was supposed to be.

He recalled Matt Shelton saying years ago that Luke's extensive podcast interview with Turney, Cornerstone's ace technical guru and restoration supervisor, was the best contribution Luke ever made to Dweeb King.

Kevin was a legend on the Cornerstone forums, and even though he and Luke never met in person, the audio conversation the two had about the challenges involved in restoring Buddy Cooper's 1945 western *Showdown at Comanche Gulch* (CS#509) was roundly lauded by those who tuned in. Somehow, a discussion about an eighty-year-old movie appealed to the *Entertainment Talk* audience who customarily didn't care about anything older than this week's nipple slip.

Placing *Forged Trenches* back where it belonged on the shelf, Luke considered a Rikard Schneider telefilm, a Denis Fontaine travelogue, and even a Pascal Caron comedy before he chose a disc from Cornerstone's *Early Hedlund* box set, *Agony* (CS#220). The description on the back of the film's case read: "A sharply sinister drama about a mysterious foreign exchange student who falls in love with her much older history professor with a checkered past."

Perfect.

Luke set his meal in front of him, soaked in the delicious glow of the crackling fire, and smiled as the CS logo on his TV set faded to black, and the film began.

Dalton would later describe this evening for Luke as *The Fall*. Every true artist, Luke's agent understood, had to, at certain points along the creative path, be forced to adapt to unforeseen circumstances, maybe even prompted to reinvent himself completely, and on this November night, Luke was forced to take a hard look into his own personal abyss.

Luke Sullivan was on the fence when it came to the vast majority of world issues both real and figurative, but there had been no doubt the man was a card-carrying Cornerstone devotee. It was his light, the apple of his eye, an incentive to constantly polish his relationship with aesthetic culture.

Agony, as it were, wasn't great. From an academic standpoint, there were identifiable motifs that would over time become branded archetypes of Hedlund's celebrated late-career masterpieces, so there was no question the film had scholarly value, but the movie was more an asterisk off to the side of the Hedlund legend than a venerated monolith in his pantheon of classics.

In a state of shock, Luke comprehended that as a professional in the field, a paid critic, he had been wrong. *Wrong*. Whether this evening of *Agony* (literally) proved he had blindly sipped Cornerstone's Kool-Aid or perhaps been momentarily mistaken as a film scholar, he had shot and missed.

The first time he saw the movie, it felt engaging in that way only initial novelty can provide, but a return trip to *Agony* left Luke stranded in forsaken new territory. How many others from the collection might inspire a similar distaste?

He knew there were Cornerstone films he wouldn't need to worry about losing faith in, but there were hundreds of movies he'd watched once, theoretically loved, and added to his library.

This epiphany throttled Luke.

Some of his Cornerstone movies might not be classics. They might instead be merely excellent or (God forbid) *pretty good*.

Busy appraising ML100 literature during the day and now recognizing a compulsion to traverse similarly through his Cornerstones at night, Luke sensed his inner cinephile mutating. Watching *Agony* severed his affiliation with the one world he thought he fully knew.

The Cornerstone Standard was fallible.

Darkness crept in.

39

"Put your back into it, you lazy pole-smoker!"

A glutton for punishment, Luke followed his Monday night Cornerstone terror with a visit to Roger's, needing to be out of the house after a dreadfully unproductive morning. He was chastised for not arriving with beers, but that didn't stop Roger from showing off the new shovel he'd bought, thrusting it into Luke's hands and insisting he return to the same deck he'd liberated from mulchy gunk three weeks earlier to purge the snow that now covered it.

Roger sat on a white plastic chair near the hot tub. "How can anyone use a tool so poorly?" he asked.

Luke leaned on the shovel. "I don't know your last name, Roger. Do you know mine?"

"Hard labor, fruitcake! Now! We're not here to have a goddamned quilting bee!"

Roger began the elaborate dance of standing up. As he slowly crept up the deck toward his front door, he pointed to Luke with his cane.

"I'm going to lie down," he said. "Don't rifle through my stuff while I'm napping. If you sniff around my hamper, I'll know!"

Luke finished an hour later, and when he peeked in on the old man, he was snoring on his recliner. He stared at Roger, cataloging physical attributes he'd never noted. Luke could spot Roger's white hair from a block away but hadn't realized he had a full five-o'clock shadow beard to match. And his inelegant flop onto the chair earlier had forced up part of his shirt, revealing the fleshy foothills of a beer gut.

When Luke tried writing again that night, he typed a multiple page description of Roger. He didn't know what value it had, or if there was a place for it in his story, but he thought his prose portrait wasn't bad.

He printed it out and taped it to his office wall.

40

Luke was a soup bigot.

As an opening act to a grander meal, he could muster a flat tolerance of the stuff, but regardless of blend or style, it had always been a food he could step away from. However, the hearty broth Anya cooked for them was a revelation. It was without question the greatest dinner Luke had eaten in four months.

If only the two of them didn't have to sit in silence while they ate.

Their routine ordinarily involved picking away at dinner on the couch in front of a movie, but tonight – their fourth date – was special for some reason. They sat at the table.

Understanding the implications of this, Luke became more than a little expectant. Was this the beginning of a true connection? Was physical intimacy imminent? Even a vague possibility of this enhanced the soup before him. Luke dug into it with the urgency of a growing teenager.

In fact, Luke's new considerations of sexual what-ifs made him feel like a 16-year-old in more ways than one. Allowing an inner photoplay to unfold (seeing as Anya never looked at him while she ate), Luke bounded in his mind back to Pedersen High School and the budding lusts he had for those lanky dream girls who inspired Luke and many of his buddies to join the drama club.

Luke's initiation didn't begin with *Licorice Dakota*'s own Roberta Davis or her hippychick gal pal Amy Wolfe, but class Lothario Greg Houser, the brooding alpha male every one of these drama ladies wanted a piece of. Houser stood six inches taller than any other guy in the class and was beefy and strong where Luke and his comrades were, let's say, *not*.

It couldn't have been only his height and build, though: Luke and his backstage crew pals spent hours discussing what gifts Greg possessed that make him such a panty-dropper.

Houser proved it to Luke and his fellow neophytes once, in a magnificent display of sexual prowess that transformed him from the drama boys' idol into a veritable figurehead of virility. Not only did he claim to have slept with Amy Wolfe, the shining star of their semester-ending variety show, but he convinced her to perform her popular lisping trash lady sketch (which Luke had helped write) wearing a black garbage bag and nothing else.

Happy to share his exploits with Luke and five equally eager stagehands, Greg directed three of them at a time (one trio on Friday night, the other on Saturday) up to the crawl space above stage right five minutes before the trash lady was set to take the stage.

Obscured by dark shadows, Luke and his pals (they insisted on being in the first wave) watched Greg enter Amy's changing room and kiss her for twenty-five seconds (Stan Briggs, squatting next to Luke, timed it with his calculator watch) before they saw her undress completely and don her trash bag.

Luke and his cronies reviewed the awesomeness of the situation with breathless enthusiasm as they watched the skit from the scaffolding, at one point spotting Greg Houser backstage, appearing very pleased with himself.

Luke returned to the present day and finished his soup.

He knew he'd seethe in romantic anguish if he didn't act, so after popping a high-concept cross-dressing comedy sequel into the DVD player, Luke took his place on the couch and channeled Greg Houser.

As she set her wine glass down on the coffee table, Luke jutted out over the center cushion and kissed Anya on the cheek. Luke steeled himself, waiting for her to respond in one way or another, but she sat still, acutely focused on the FBI Warning playing on the screen.

Soon, though, he felt her lips on his own cheek. Before long, they were kissing timidly and tenderly, a vomiting movie star in drag dancing on the TV across the room.

41

He had danced around it for months, but when he found himself beating his head against a chapter that wouldn't come together, Luke knew he needed to do something drastic to get his juices flowing again.

He decided to write while drunk.

Luke told Ray about it during their afternoon chat.

Ray: *I couldn't do my job hammered. I'd just fall asleep.*

Luke: *We've watched movies while sloshed before, right? Why not try writing that way?*

Ray: *If even in a minor way you're getting paid to be loaded, you are my hero.*

Luke: *Your support means everything.*

Luke knew this writing test had the potential to fail miserably, but he'd just finished *Under the Volcano*, which was a novel stunningly soaked in firewater, and he figured that while in a wine-induced creative trajectory, he might discover an uncultivated command of the language.

He had fallen in love with the central character in his novel, Daylin Hensley, a free-spirited mother of four who secretly loathed the life she'd carved out for herself. Her husband was all right, the kids were fine, and her job passed the time, but something snaps in her. As Daylin's mental existence splinters, the mystery behind the novel's centerpiece murder and subsequent courtroom drama comes to light.

Luke didn't want to finesse a plot point or stay specific: he needed to dive into his protagonist's head. His current scuffle with Cornerstone was likely fueling this fascination with his character's uneasy ties to the world, but didn't want to get too intellectual about it. He downed a third glass of wine and sat at his desk.

Luke was excited to instigate this adventure, and as he laughed out loud when referring to it as *lit*erature, he knew he was soused enough to begin.

I wish I could think in French. Or better yet, a secret code language only I knew. When the silver spaceship lands, and I hope it comes soon, I want to be first to see our new friends, and I don't want anyone but me to understand them.

One quick second where it's mine and mine alone.

Nah, fuck whatever psychic beeps and clicks these aliens use to communicate. I want a secret. I don't have any left. I've given all my secrets to Barry and the kids.

Is there really nothing of my own?

Here's something.

When I walk across the 7th Street Bridge, at the same point every time, I feel the urge to jump. I don't want to die; I want to fly. I bet death hurts. Maybe alien cultures have solved death, and when they arrive, they'll share that with us.

Great. The aliens have a juicy secret, and I don't.

I thought about this the other night. I don't know why anyone would be interested, but for what it's worth, no one's heard this one. Barry told me on our honeymoon that his favorite parts of my body were my breasts. I lied and said I liked his arms.

The truth is that the furry tuft of hair right above his ass drives me wild. I don't have a desire to touch it, but it makes frumpy Barry seem like a beast. Those nights he sleeps with his shirt off, I stare at it. It's different than what used to be on Barry's head, more like thick doll hair. He'll ruin these moments by farting or snoring, but I still peek whenever I have a chance.

Is there a French term for this part of the body? If there is, I bet the aliens know about it.

After reading this the next morning, Luke swiped all evidence of Daylin's sensual inner song.

Only sober writing from now on, he thought.

42

Luke started watching John Garfield freak out on a pill-popping bender in *Last Exit* (CS#570) after dinner, learning early in this second viewing that it fell into the same camp as Hedlund's *Agony*. It was sometimes excellently odd, but it felt less vital and dangerous than it did the night its beautiful Cornerstone Standard screener arrived at the Dweeb King office. Luke was snoozing on the couch before it was halfway over, and at 10:00 pm, he turned off the TV and stumbled down the stairs.

He shook off his jeans, kicked them toward the closet door, and removed his shirt so violently he almost ripped it. Angry the pants he'd thrown off were now making it difficult to open his closet, he grunted a few choice sentence fragments and finally gained access to his dresser and, inside it, his pajama bottoms.

At first, he thought it was a fluffy, multicolored cat toy, something left behind by one of the cabin's previous tenants. Luke almost didn't notice when the chipmunk spat to life, zooming in a frenzy into the deep recesses of the closet.

Luke stepped away as quietly as his body would allow. He grabbed his bedspread and inched back into the hall, shutting the bedroom door silently, sealing this chipmunk outbreak before it spread any further.

Coming up with the airtight logical reasoning that no critter could assault him if he slept on the kitchen table, Luke took a series of uncomfortable elevated cat naps there through the night and woke up with a backache that made him feel eighty years old. He flicked on the coffee maker, threw a piece of bread in the toaster, and considered the controversy at hand.

Though nothing was damaged, everything had changed.

What Luke found on the internet was a grotesquery of sickeningly detailed means to murder the critters. The quickest annihilation involved a mousetrap loaded with a piece of cheese (or, as one expert wrote, the fuckers loved peanut butter), but there was a plethora of distinctly more sadistic methods of offing the varmints that Luke investigated thoroughly.

The most complexly medieval setup consisted of a bucket, a gallon of water, and a yardstick. According to the psycho who posted the how-to manual, you fill the bucket with water (hot water, for some ghastly reason) and lay a light saucer carrying a spoonful of peanut butter on top of the liquid as far from the bucket's rim as possible.

Next, you construct a ramp with your yardstick so the dumb chumps can walk on up to the rim of the bucket only to find themselves incapable of saying no to the peanut butter. They'd maybe enjoy a bite or two of their feast as they drowned. Luke relished the idea of committing chipmunk-cide, but he lacked the constitution to embark on blood-letting this depraved.

He drove forty miles to the only hardware store in the area that carried the SPCA-approved Chipmunk Diversion Device, which a salesman implored Luke not to waste his money on. It was basically the same setup as the bucket apparatus, just without the water torture at the end.

The CDD was a metal cage with a collapsible door and a ramp built into its frame. Once the animal made it far enough inside toward the tasty foodstuff at the device's heart, its weight would trigger the outer door shut, trapping it. This would provide Luke the opportunity – or, as it was phrased in advertisements, the *privilege* – to relocate the bastard far, far away.

While the hardware store salesman couldn't keep Luke from buying the kooky gadget, he at least convinced him to pick up some run-of-the-mill mousetraps as a precaution.

It took Luke two hours to construct the CDD in his kitchen, an eternity. But an enthusiastic paranoia kept him pushing ever forward: he wanted to prove to Alvin or Theodore he meant business. When the creation of this chipmunk Death Star was complete, he ladled a liberal mountain of peanut butter into the proper receptacle deep within the CDD. He set it in front of his bedroom and opened the airlocked chamber, terrified it was going to scamper out toward him.

Luke then wondered how to pass the time waiting for this hungry hungry chipmunk to come a-courtin'. His rodent mania would keep him from harnessing enough focus to write, but he couldn't clean or do other chores because he didn't want any noise distracting the animal from its impending demise. He opted to type up his notes from the last couple days, monitoring the CDD frequently from the next room.

Hours passed.

Luke, his crazy having flared with chipmunk fury, switched from typing his notes to reading them while sitting near the bathroom at the end of the hall, insistent he be present whenever it decided to show up.

And there it was.

The animal surveyed the scene. It moved sporadically, standing motionless before zipping to its next location with a convulsive shake, causing Luke's heart to stop with every dogleg. Finally, the chipmunk crossed the threshold of the CDD.

The only sounds Luke registered were the hoarse wheezes of his own breathing.

The chipmunk zigzagged up the metal ramp and, as the CDD instruction manual had promised, began feasting on the peanut butter.

No trigger was released, no doors slammed. Luke knew that even if he dashed with ninja stealth and pulled the damned trap door himself, the increasingly well-fed rodent would bolt back into the bedroom before he got to it. Luke had to stay where he was and pray one of the chipmunk's jerks would prompt the CDD's door to seal its fate.

Luke Sullivan watched that chipmunk lick the peanut butter at the sensor core of the expensive contraption until it was all gone. It then nonchalantly turned around and whisked out of the CDD, back into his bedroom.

Luke got up, pulled the bedroom door shut, and went to get the mousetraps.

43

The first statement from Shelton during their weekly Dweeb King chat that Friday was, "Could you give me your agent's phone number? I have a great book idea."

There was no easy way to wriggle around this kind of no-win conversation starter. You were a jerk if you let somebody know you had no intention of sharing valuable contact info, and you were a liar if you offered a vague half-truth like, "Give me a synopsis, and we'll see what we can do."

And fuck Shelton for dropping this on Luke so purposefully early. This was supposed to be a tidy recap of the ins and outs of the website and its TV counterpart, and any unnecessary discussion meant more time dealing with Kisser, which was cruel and unusual punishment.

"Why don't we talk about this after the meeting?"

Shelton said, "You could type it to me in a message. That would be fine."

Changing the topic, Luke asked, "What's this I hear about some of the guys changing positions?"

Shelton had one last contribution on the subject. "We're going to return to this," he said. "It's important to me."

Luke didn't respond.

Shelton monotonously kicked into work mode. "TV ratings are way down," he said.

"Why do we think they're so low?"

"The demographic we need to lock down doesn't watch shows like *Entertainment Talk* anymore," Shelton said. "We need to establish more of an online video presence."

"I bet everyone agrees with you. How should we get going on that?"

"Well, our publicist resigned."

"We have a publicist?"

"Had."

"Is it worth paying a professional PR person?" Luke asked. "We should utilize our in-house guys for that, don't you think?"

"I changed Evan's title from VP to publicist a month ago, and it turned out he wasn't interested in appealing to the audiophile and gear publications I think have the best opportunities for us, so we parted ways."

"Evan *quit?*"

"Koji and Clyde are leaving, too," Shelton added.

"That's half our executive payroll," Luke screamed. "I'm just hearing about this now? Why didn't you run this past me?"

"I didn't want to," he said. "Didn't need to."

Luke knew if he threw a fit at this juncture, it would come back to bite him in the ass, so he sat on the six or seven choice names he wanted to call Shelton. It was Luke's fault for leaving the company if he cared as much about it as he felt like he did at the moment, but that didn't stop the angry sentiment from melting through his veins.

Luke swore he heard a sly snort in Shelton's voice before Kisser asked, "Have you heard the expression that sometimes it's easier to ask for forgiveness than permission?"

This wasn't a check-in call. It was a checkmate move in a chess game, and Luke was unprepared. "How different would this conversation have been if I had given you my agent's info when you asked for it?" Luke asked.

"I hope your novel is coming along well," Shelton said.

The meeting was over. And, it seemed, so was Dweeb King.

44

There was a woman in Luke's college dorm who tended bar twice a week. Her biggest pet peeve was patrons ordering glasses of wine. If you cared enough to go to a wine bar or a fancy gala, that was all fine and good, but she'd insist to Luke and his floormates when they'd stop by her establishment for a Tuesday nightcap that a meaningful saloon mantra was this:

Never drink wine at a bar.

This memory came to him at Keene's, prompted by the fellow playing video poker next to Luke who offered to buy everyone in the place a round, having hit some kind of jackpot. It was a slow night at the restaurant, with some of the usual crowd milling around, and Marion and his obnoxious girlfriend busy necking in a distant booth. Even Misty's presence was minimal, seeing as she was off doing inventory with the owners.

The video poker champion at Luke's left was so excited about his win that he forced Luke to put down his library copy of *Parade's End* by Ford Madox Ford and get soaked with him in celebration. Jeremy was a goofy Midwesterner who had moved to Deer Meadow a decade earlier to ski, and was working part-time at Keene's (on Misty's days off).

He kept banging his leg brace against the inside of the bar. Jeremy had jacked it on the slopes the first day of the season – he called it a *major bummer*, thick with bodacious snow-dude lilt – and bemoaned the shredding he was missing out on.

Luke mentioned his old buddy and her no-wine bar edict, and Jeremy, reminding Luke he was a bartender himself, brushed it off, insisting Luke drink what he wanted. Feeling local, Luke reached across the bar to an open bottle of Cabernet, poured the beer out of his pint glass into a nearby sink, and filled it tall with vino.

Misty walked over, on one of her intermittent rounds. "Please," she said. "Help yourself."

With the hooch on heavy flow, Luke and Jeremy dug deep into a long conversation, one that spent its first cycle introducing biographical backgrounds, occupations, and girlfriends, and before they knew it, another wine bottle had been opened, and Misty found herself bringing two beers at a time for Jeremy.

After an hour of this, while Misty wouldn't have registered the name, she surely could pinpoint the slurred speech of Blotto.

"I mean, how would *you* describe it?" he demanded.

"I don't even know where to start, man."

"Exactly!" Blotto exclaimed. "I have characters who are all over one another, but every time I try to get into the moment, it sounds stupid."

"What about your girl?" Jeremy asked. "Take one of your nights together and write that as a scene."

"The woman who doesn't speak any English?" he asked. "Yeah, that one's swarming with good dialogue."

Blotto called Jeremy to action. The wine had made him bold. "Okay," he said. "What words work in a sex scene?"

Jeremy stared down at his brace as Luke, with a devilish fire that was bound to get him in trouble, asked, "*Pussy?*"

"Sure."

"*Intercourse?*"

"Probably not."

"*Fucking?*"

Misty, overhearing these shenanigans, couldn't resist. "Y'all are fucking without me?"

"I'm trying to figure out what words to use in my book," Blotto said. "*Banging?*"

"Why not keep it simple?" Misty asked. "*Making love?*"

Jeremy and Luke jeered in unison, provoking guffaws, and Misty decided if she was going to keep talking with these yahoos, she'd need a shot or three.

What followed was a lively discussion that lasted until closing time. Jeremy and Misty gave Luke a parade of flowery words that in one way or another had something to do with the physical act of love, but as Blotto careened into and through his third bottle of cheap Cabernet, he was of no mind to fully classify these contributions.

Blotto begged Misty to let him sleep in a booth, but she wouldn't have it. Jeremy's place was around the corner from Keene's, so Luke took the first leg of his journey home with his new pal's arm keeping him steady in the snow. From there, he ventured off alone and was so bombed that when he got home, he slept soundly in his bedroom, not remembering his roommate the chipmunk.

45

PORTNOY'S COMPLAINT

PHILIP ROTH
1969

ML#52

monologue of a guy talking to
his shrink

- autobiography? Is Roth really
like this?

- Are his great sex scenes
or terrible ones?

"But I don't need dreams, Doctor
that's why I hardly leave
them - because I have this life
instead."

NATIONAL BOOK AWARD x2

PULITZER for

AMERICAN PASTORAL 1997

GROCERIES (coffee)

chicken breasts
wine vegetable.

46

Where they had burst at their seams upon Luke's arrival in Deer Meadow, in the days leading up to Thanksgiving, Luke's DVD shelves looked like they had been looted. A messy stack of rejects had taken over a corner of the living room, one-time favorites that had been ceremonially exempted from their once heralded statuses.

Luke hadn't talked to Anya since Thursday (Marion assured him it was a busy time for them at the casino), but even if she had been available, the prospect of sex took a distant second when it came to the upkeep of Luke's meticulously thorough spreadsheet he had designed for his project. In a fleeting Dweeb King flashback, Luke thought it might make a great *Entertainment Talk* segment, though he was quick to let that idea rest in peace.

As a rule, when the sun went down – Luke's go-to signal it was time to stop writing – he would start his next trial by fire, inserting a Cornerstone disc into his Blu-ray player and seeing whether it retained its classic stature. Only towering masterpieces remained: if you were merely *interesting*, you were sent to the trenches with the rest of the meat.

He anticipated that some of tonight's choices would remain in his arsenal (it took ten short minutes of Barry Nicosia's *Scandal* (CS#173) for him to remember how glorious it was), but he figured at least one or two were headed to the guillotine.

He logged a degree of concern when it was time for *3.14* (CS #404). Like so many other of his fellow students at film school, he was drawn to Angelo Ricci's venerated oeuvre. The loopier, more metafilmic designs he concocted toward the end of his career were often too heady and impenetrable for their own good (*City of Lights* (CS#571) was especially obtuse), but *3.14* connected with him intensely... that one time he watched it.

The opening dream sequence was famously provocative, an introduction that served as a clarion example of the power of moviemaking: it was a mainstay in first-year film classes. But Luke was anxious the flaring excitement of this prologue would wane as the movie played on, and with the needlessly strict rules in this experiment of his, a deduction from classic to excellent was the equivalent of a death sentence.

He breathed deeply when *3.14* was better than ever – beginning, middle, and end alike. Luke thought to himself for a while after finishing it that he needed to be careful not to approach this Cornerstone endeavor as a quest for perfection. As *3.14* hit its final notes, Luke calmly considered that as exceptional as the film was, it wasn't perfect at all.

Writing this on one of his notepads, he knew the sentiment stunk like a double-speak dum-dum life lesson, but the sparkle within Ricci's blissfully strong movie wasn't reliant on precise technical exactness. There was more to it. This opened another trap door – if Luke, in his search for classic cinema, wasn't striving for perfect grace, what was he chasing?

All heartache aside, he was convinced he was having the time of his life.

47

He was the only member of his immediate family who could remember his dreams. Luke maybe couldn't recall their comprehensive symbolism, but he had relatively easy mental access to the images his sleeping excursions inspired. In another of his undertakings meant to kickstart his creative drive, Luke decided he would harness this spirit of his, to see what kind of insights existed within the murky depths of his subconscious.

He was going to take the chore of communication out of the equation. No contributions from the waking world. Luke was going to lasso the primordial authenticity at the root of his inner self.

He hated the idea that the notepad on the table next to his bed could be accurately referred to as a dream journal, but that's what it was. Luke prepared a second pad on a bookshelf near the couch, in case a nap in the middle of the afternoon generated dancing apparitions in his mind that were worth noting.

Over the course of the week, though, these lures he cast into the oceans of dreamscapes didn't get any bites. It wasn't until a mild Friday that transmissions from the ether arrived.

Whatever it was that aroused such psychic storm clouds, Luke found himself in a trance that was thunderously intense. If the chipmunk in Luke's closet (still untended to, presently forgotten about) had been listening, it might have heard the groans and troubled breathing that had taken sleeping Luke over, body and spirit.

After riding his head trip like a bucking bronco, Luke

seized to life, jolting upright in his bed. There was no moon in the sky, so even with all the reflective snow on the ground, blackness abounded. Without a light on, he couldn't see a thing. Quivering from the repercussions of what had roared through his mind, a sliver of consciousness silently bit Luke, reminding him of the notepad near his bed.

Luke fumbled for pen and paper and wrote furiously in longhand, elated he'd finally found the opportunity to chronicle these deep-sea visions that had eluded him for so long. He scratched away, describing what was still so visible and present to him.

He channeled the void. This was the great dialogue. From his dream world through his pen, he had perceived his most basic psychogenic truths.

- -

Luke felt like a child on Christmas morning as he reached for the notepad the next day. He flipped it over to take a look, brimming with not-yet-caffeinated excitement.

A peal of unease ripped through him. This was no Rosetta Stone offering a primer to the mystery of his sleeping mind, no recollection of a journey past the threshold of dreams.

It was, as it turned out, gibberish.

Page one contained the drawing of a trapezoid and some curlicues. The next showcased crudely-colored oval shapes followed by zigzags that ventured out from the pad's center in every direction. Page three had four dots on it, nothing more. Page seven was crowded with smiley faces.

What Luke had scribbled were banal hieroglyphics, what a first-grader would doodle on the cover of a school folder.

A follow-up wave of terror then crested over him: what

if these codes were the results of impulses sent into his brain by his cabin's ghost? If he were to decipher this beyond-language script, what horrors would he unveil?

He didn't want to know. The dream journals were recycled into the fire that night.

48

Anya didn't seem interested in dinner. The way she held herself as they sat quietly in the kitchen that evening made it appear as though she was wrestling with a killer headache. After leaving her with a DVD to watch on her own, she thrilled Luke by attempting to say his name as he stepped out into the night. It came out of her mouth like a breathy whisper, and once their lingering goodnight kiss came to an end, her hand drifted from his shoulder to his wrist with a demure flit.

This was all Luke could ponder while writing and (mostly) pacing the next afternoon. Realizing Anya had left a major mark on him without the use of language, Luke sifted through the sands of his mind for truly intense nonverbal emotional interactions he'd had in the past, ones where his precious words didn't provide any structure or disclaimer.

Falling into memory, he was transported to the frenzy of the Sullivan house in the summertime, where a ten-year-old Luke and his brothers helped mom and dad pack for a vacation. Plants were watered, suitcases were zipped up, and Luke's dad and his brother Brian were busy strapping giant boxes on top of the car (*B-Town!*, he thought).

Luke's task was to make sure Toothpaste the cat had food and water enough to last her through the weekend. A hand-me-down from a neighbor's unwanted litter that in a moment of weakness Luke's mom couldn't resist adopting, Toothpaste was hands-off to a fault. She'd warm up cozily to whichever Sullivan served her food at meal time, but Toothpaste mostly kept to herself, roaming the property, her own boss, fuck you very much.

The cat wasn't holed up in her usual haunt in Luke's newly-accessed recollection. She had a clear preference for one corner of the tool shed out back that got sunlight throughout the day. The woodpile out by the fence was another favorite retreat, but Toothpaste wasn't there, either. As Luke continued his perimeter of the Sullivan compound, he finally saw the cat near a tree.

Luke approached Toothpaste, repeating her name, but she never acknowledged him. When he knelt down and touched her, he felt a tumultuous, racing heartbeat beneath her wispy hair.

Running toward the house with the animal, it felt to Luke felt like Toothpaste had a horrific gyroscope spinning too fast under her skin. He alerted his parents, and, postponing the onset of their journey (to the chagrin of his older brothers), Luke and his mom and dad loaded Toothpaste into the truck and headed to the vet.

Luke knew when the animal doctor's once-over in that sterile examination room took less than thirty seconds the diagnosis would be bad. The decision was quickly made to put her down. Toothpaste had suffered an attack, probably a stroke, and the vet gave the Sullivans a minute to say their goodbyes.

Mr. Sullivan squeezed the animal tenderly, somber with the realization the fleabag would no longer be a walking garden presence at their home. Even Luke's feline-hating mother placed a calm hand on the beast's back, whispering, "So it goes, you stupid cat."

Toothpaste didn't meow or purr at all. She only shook with discomfort, likely deaf, dumb, and blind. When Luke leaned down to caress her, unsure what message he wanted to send the cat to the great beyond with, she turned her head in a fast swish, and they locked eyes.

Whether or not she was staring at him, Luke wasn't sure, but the two of them held this exchange for a long while. Toothpaste peered at him, into him, through him, something.

She did this until the vet took the animal away.

Luke cried loudly, unafraid of embarrassing himself in the solitude of his cabin. It had been so long he couldn't remember exactly what the cat looked like, but the love he felt for Toothpaste had been real. She might not have given a shit about him, but he invested his heart in that beloved pet. Here was the sincere non-language connection he'd been trying to track down.

Thanks, Toothpaste. Ride the lightning.

49

"What would it take to convince you," Luke asked, "to tell me your biggest secret?"

Luke and his Romanian pal sat at a picnic table on Keene's back patio. The heat of Marion's cigar glowed in the twilight, its smoke slowly wafting into the sky. He'd brought an extra one for Luke, who was positive he was smoking it wrong.

Marion gave the impression he was mulling over Luke's cheesy question, which Luke had posed after struggling all afternoon with Daylin Hensley and her fictional difficulties coming to terms with the enigmas of the world. Signaling a clear break in whatever contemplation he'd staged, Marion shook his head and tapped cigar ash into the snow.

"Your novel is going to be filled with sissies who don't shut up," Marion said. "You must focus on mystery. What is NOT spoken."

"Gee, thanks, Lobo."

"Intrigue! Suspense!" Marion yelled. "These things start fires! They make babies laugh! They cause erections to grow five times their normal size!"

As though he'd inspired himself with this sexually fantastical descriptor, Marion rested his cigar on the table and rushed into the restaurant. Luke watched him slip behind the bar like he owned the place to snag a pen and some order slips.

Upon Marion storming back outside, Misty said, "You two sweethearts are going to freeze your nuts off out there!"

Marion grabbed his cigar and began tearing the papers into small scraps. "My father did this for me when I went off to university."

"You told me you didn't go to college," Luke replied.

"I didn't," Marion said coolly, pushing a pen and torn shreds toward his friend. "This is a great lesson. You will take me seriously."

Marion wrote on a slip of paper and folded it up. "This is how you free yourself from the past," he said. "On this is something I don't want anyone to know. I'd shame my family if even a stranger were to see."

Marion then put it on the lit end of his cigar. It took a second for the material to catch, but when it did, that sucker turned to ash.

"Now it is no more," Marion said, swishing his whiskey around. "Only women share secrets out loud. It's a character flaw."

An instant passed in silence as Luke prepared a fiery campaign of mockery against this ludicrously new-age act. Before he had a chance to speak, Marion flicked his cigar and punched Luke on the shoulder.

"Just kidding," he said. "That never happened. But you can have it for your book."

50

Luke's grandmother was a powderkeg. Toni (*Not short for anything!*, if you ever asked) had the lungs of a Broadway star and the stature of an unassuming gypsy. She'd come across meekly upon first impression, but once she considered the ice broken, Toni would gab until somebody had the guts to shut her up.

Luke assumed it was Dalton calling surprisingly early at 7:00 am, but it was his mom alerting him that Toni had suffered a minor heart attack. It was Sunday evening by the time Luke arrived at the hospital, and stepping into Toni's room, he saw a Catholic priest there with her, reading from a hymnal.

She didn't greet Luke at all, too busy focusing on the God talk underway. In fact, the first time Toni actively looked at Luke that night was when the priest got out his Eucharistic tools. She asked Luke in language that was more thought-out and controlled than her usual throaty epithets: "Care to join me?"

As sassy and callous as Toni could sometimes be, whenever it came to the man upstairs, she was concentrated and contrite. Toni was a bullshitter supreme, but any time even a Catholic-adjacent topic was raised, she would speak as though she was offering a humbled prayer. This devotion radiated from her blue eyes toward Luke, who didn't say a word.

The priest added, "All are welcome."

Luke shook his head.

Regaining a sliver of her trademark fire, Toni glanced back to the priest. "Kids these days, huh?" she asked.

The minute the priest left the room, Toni pointed to a chair close to her bed. There was a distinct pattern to their greeting – Luke would put his right cheek to Toni's lips, and she'd give him a quick peck.

"When are you back?" she asked. "West Virginia is kinda dumb, isn't it?"

"It ain't too bad," Luke said.

Toni swatted at him. "You sound like a Southerner. Go back to New York and get a job. You're not even married. It's embarrassing."

She sat up and changed the channel on her TV, finding a game show and muting the set with her oversized remote control.

"These doctors know nothing," Toni said. "They're all pharmacy school dropouts."

Not entirely breaking concentration with the television in the background, Toni added, "You're seeing someone, I hope."

"Pardon?" Luke asked, missing her question.

"I figure if you're dating now, a wedding in a year isn't out of the picture, then a great-grandchild the year after."

"You're so greedy," Luke said. "You have litters of great-grandkids already."

She slapped him again. "My beautiful great-grandsons weren't born in a cardboard box under the stairs."

"Oh, right," Luke said. "You want one of us to have a girl."

Another whack, this time at something invisible in front of her. "Too many boys already," she said.

She turned the volume back up on the TV and the two of them watched the rest of the show.

51

Luke opened his parents' front door and saw Pam, martini in hand, yelling at his father behind her. "I swear to God she's going to sell it for cult money! You might as well give it away."

Exhausted from what appeared to be a marathon quarrel, Luke's dad took off his glasses and made two cocktails at the bar – a medium-sized drink for Luke and a bigger one for himself. Pam wasted no time shoehorning Luke into the hotbed with them.

"You should see your grandmother in the morning," she said. "She is not long for this world."

"It's best if we stay calm about this," Kyle responded.

Ferocious with a steaming anger, Pam screamed, "She will *not* leave that hospital alive. Not with your sisters acting the way they are."

She turned back to Luke. "They have been *awful.*"

Pam set her empty glass on the counter near Kyle. "First thing tomorrow. Go see her."

"I just did," Luke said.

"When?"

"An hour ago."

Kyle, desperate to recruit Luke to his side of the scene, asked, "How did she look to you?"

"Fine," Luke said, happy staying out of it.

"Mark my words," Pam said. "She's a goner."

Maybe two minutes were spent in passive-aggressive discourse regarding Pam's thoughts on Luke getting too skinny, but the rest of the evening's deliberations involved Toni. The three Sullivans wearied themselves so thoroughly talking about her that by 9:00 pm, Pam and Kyle retired for the night, leaving Luke to his own devices.

He wandered the halls of his old Altoona home, ultimately arriving at what his brothers had designated the Wall of Shame. The far side of the family room was dedicated to photos of the Sullivan clan through the decades (though Pam would be quick to note that a wall in the living room was devoted exclusively to pictures of grandsons).

He scanned an image of Pam giving a speech at the mayor's office, his brother John catching a game-winning football pass, and ultimately a portrait of himself. His dad had always referred to it as Luke *ruining film*: he had a habit of opening his mouth and making a face in most photos taken of him. He didn't know when the pattern started (or why, for that matter), but here on the Wall of Shame, most snapshots of Luke showcased this idiocy.

There was one exception: Luke's senior high school portrait that Ray nicknamed The Dragonslayer.

Reappraising the photo, Luke realized there were thousands of things wrong with it. The smokiness to its heavily textured faux-forest backdrop. And the clothing – brand new sandals worn with white tube socks and the famous Ethnic Vest. Luke had discovered the orange and black depiction of cave-dwelling natives on his first unsupervised trip to New York City, where the woman who sold it to him assured him it had been crafted by Peruvian nomads. He tore out its *Made in China* tag when he got it home.

Then (*Dear God*, Luke thought) there were the glasses. Once he learned the value of contact lenses, Luke never looked back, but in the years before this discovery, he sported spectacles that appeared to be the better part of an inch thick, a girth barely contained by the Buddy Holly rims Luke loved at the time.

His face, however, was the true delicacy of The Dragonslayer. Luke expected that at some point in his life he'd stop being embarrassed by the *Who farted?* expression he wore in the picture, but tonight, he was as ashamed as ever.

To the right of the Dragonslayer, Luke recognized a photo he had never seen on the Walk of Shame. He snapped it three years ago during Pam's run for a seat on Blair County's board of supervisors.

It had been a backbreaking campaign, and after investing endless hours and way more money than she planned on burning though, Pam lost by a paper-thin margin, and Luke, his brother Brian, and Kyle stayed up all night with her after final vote counts came in.

Here she was: Pam on the back porch, coffee mug in front of her, the sun threatening to rise, a bittersweet smile on her face.

In the morning, Kyle announced he had to be in Dallas for a week starting Monday. Not thinking she'd agree to it, Luke asked Pam if she wanted to tool around Deer Meadow for a day. She refused to come anywhere near B-Town, but by lunch, a plane flight was booked.

52

Contrary to Pam's prophecy of death and ruin, Toni was back at her condo two days later. The nurse from the hospital recommended hiring a caregiver, but if there indeed had been woods, Toni was now out of them.

After one last grandma fly-by, Luke was off to the Powells'. Within ninety seconds of entering the place, Luke found himself nestled on their couch, beer in hand, talking with Lori about some new toys.

For a fleeting moment, there was no book to write, no girlfriend to worry about, no life questions tapping on the back doors of his mind. Before long, this temporary freedom from the rigors of the world made Luke sleepy.

As he drifted off, Lori said, "You're not listening."

Jolting out of his restful interlude, Luke picked up a doll Lori had been describing.

"That's Carmen," she said.

Luke pointed at the doll's leopard-print tutu. "What does Carmen do for a living that she can dress like this?"

"I don't know."

"If you were a banker or a lawyer, you probably couldn't get away with wearing a bikini or whatever this is at work," Luke asked.

"I like her outfit," Lori said confidently. "It's cute."

"Does Carmen work from home?" he asked. "Maybe she telecommutes. That'd explain things."

Nicole chortled to herself in the kitchen nearby.

"Carmen does *not* telecommute," Lori said.

"Do you even know what that word means?"

"Of course I know what it means."

"Prove it."

"*You* prove it!"

Luke set his beer down, getting serious. The smile on Lori's face was a mile wide. "True or false: I'm telecommuting right now," he said.

"False!"

"That's actually correct. Good job."

Lori bolted upright, energized by this exchange.

"My turn," she said. "True or false: I'm telecommuting right now."

With fireball enthusiasm, she thrust herself into a handstand. *"TELECOMMUTING! ARE YOU READY TO ROCK?"*

Luke tickled her, prompting her to screech loudly. He threw her over his shoulder and walked into the dining room for dinner.

"You understand, right?"

Luke had wondered where Ray had been keeping himself. It turned out he had a piece of news he wasn't too keen on sharing with his houseguest, so he did geocaching research in the garage all afternoon, knowing Luke and the girls would be fine on their own. They spent ten minutes discussing why the Patriots were better than the Packers over dinner, but it wasn't until they lounged in the living room after doing the dishes that the real business of the hour presented itself.

"Have I been doing a bad job?"

Nicole said, "Lori *loves* Uncle Luke."

"That's why we need to get Travis in there," Ray said. "We want him to have a chance to be to Dee who you are to Lori. We were going to tell you when we first changed our minds, but this is the kind of thing you say face to face, don't you think? I mean, you're still part of the family."

"Uncle Luke's birthday is on this year's calendar, you'll see," Nicole said.

This gave Luke a brief rush. The Powell family calendar, one of many gifts Ray gave his wife every Christmas, was a mainstay of their kitchen, and as meager as it was, the fact that Luke's day of birth was not written on as a reminder but was genuinely printed into the graphic design of the calendar inspired in him what must have been earnest pride.

"Do we need to hug this out or anything?" Ray said.

Luke took a long look at his best friend. Most of the time Ray came across as a grown-up, but at the moment, he very well could have been that nine-year-old who played t-ball with Luke so many decades ago.

Luke slapped him on the knee. "We're good," he said.

"Then we gotta watch *SportsCenter* and see if that d-bag from the Dodgers got traded."

It wasn't until after sundown that Luke and B-Town hit the road. Two hours out of town, he realized he hadn't told the Powells about his attempt to get a progress report from Pastor Mangi on his godfather performance. He made the executive decision after stopping for more coffee that he wouldn't ever share this with them. He'd tell Lori when she turned twenty-one, maybe.

Dreaming that Anya was pregnant made for an uneasy, tormented sleep. The last image he had before waking up was her giving birth to *Joie de vivre* (CS#539) on Blu-ray.

Luke proudly cut the umbilical cord.

53

When winter is at its zenith, there are those who dread the season's fully-formed force, preferring the open-window simplicity of sunnier days. Every time Luke Sullivan heard a wind gust or comparable agent of imminent weather, however, he hoped it was the big one. If his power got knocked out, he would have a pass to avoid typing on his computer, to walk away from work for a moment.

His wish came true late on a Thursday. He had been in a flow, getting to the heart of a chapter, when a flash switched off every piece of equipment in the house with a chirp. He'd likely lose several pages of material, but Luke was thankful for the break.

Keene's was packed that night, the storm having shut down every power grid in Deer Meadow. Generator abuzz, the restaurant was hopping. Luke was first to arrive, and within thirty minutes Marion joined him at the bar, and by the time Roger showed up, the troglodyte Kristina and Anya were also in boozy attendance.

Roger wasn't so much interested in a social drink as he was hopeful Misty's television sets were still airing the hockey game that had gone into overtime when his went dark. As she assured him he was all set up, Roger caught a glimpse of a sloshed Luke, surprised to see the guy's arm draped around a cute young thing.

Disinterested in the rowdy Romanians at their end of the bar, Roger threw Luke a big wave and walked to a less-populated section of the restaurant where he could get a private view of one of Keene's many TV sets. As he sat down, Roger couldn't help but see Luke pulling on his partner's arm, trying to get her to break away from the crowd. Anya showcased resistance to this, but they headed Roger's way anyway, Luke bumping chairs and barstools in the process.

"Roger! How are you doing?" Luke asked loudly.

Anya whispered in Romanian and squirmed out of Luke's half-embrace. She popped a quick smile to Roger and walk-skipped back over to her friends. Luke made motions like he was going to join Roger, which prompted the old man to stick his arm out and stop him.

"I'm in the market for a quiet bowl of soup and this hockey game. That's it."

"I'll only talk with you for, like, a minute," Luke said, stammering.

"You've been working hard today, I see."

This triggered a speech from Blotto that Roger tuned out. He didn't even try giving the guy the false impression he was even marginally considering this drunken buffoon's ramblings. He sipped a bottle of beer and ordered some clam chowder from Misty, only partly paying attention to Blotto when, during a commercial break, he stared over at Anya and referred to her as "the redwood of my own Romanian forest, a flower in my heart."

By the time the Flyers won, the Romanians were long gone, and Blotto had fallen asleep at the bar next to Roger. Jeremy was the only other drinker left in the place. Roger left cash for Misty and asked whether power was back on in town.

"My buddy texted and said it's on, at least on Northwood," Jeremy said.

"Rockin' good news," Roger said.

Jeremy put on the kindest voice he could muster under the heavy cloak of vodka tonics. "Can I bum a ride home from you?" he asked.

"I walked."

Misty pointed to the drooling, sleeping dweeb. "Maybe y'all should leave together," she said. "Easier to carry him that way."

Roger and Jeremy slogged through the snow under a sea of moonlight, Luke's limp body between them. They attempted conversation as they left the restaurant, but ran out of shared interests after only a few paces. Halfway up the hill to Luke's cabin, Jeremy broke the silence.

"Is it true his place is haunted?" he asked. Roger, winded, didn't recognize this stupidity with a response of any kind. "Has he ever mentioned anything to you?"

Roger grunted, "Nope."

The crunch of ice was a metronome beneath their feet.

"I don't want to go inside," Jeremy decreed. "He can keep his ghosts to himself."

Jeremy kept his word and bolted once he and Roger hauled Luke up the steps to his front door. Roger leaned against the railing, impressed he'd been able to get all the way there without having a coronary. Luke was unconscious, so Roger found himself participating in the most unintentionally homoerotic moment of his life as his fished through the catatonic writer's front pockets for house keys.

Roger didn't even take Luke's shoes off as he shoved him onto his unmade bed. Sleepy himself, Roger decided to nap on Luke's couch before braving the night air again. But after he climbed the stairs and took a load off, Roger heard something.

It wasn't the rodent scratching he'd been alerted to during his last visit – this was a voice, a creepy, stilted screaming.

Did Luke have a ghost?

What he spotted on the far side of Luke's fireplace was a mouse trap with a shockingly large chipmunk caught in its sprung metal death grip. Roger switched on the living room light and the creature's last ditch efforts at freeing itself became more intense: the critter wasn't about to leave this realm without a fight. With unnerving volume and thrash, both the chipmunk and the trap that was killing it flailed from one side of the room to the other, whimpering with high-pitched discomfort.

Roger went home, happy to leave this animal control issue to the wino downstairs.

54

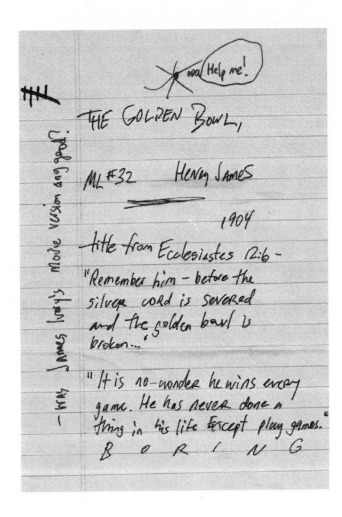

55

He sent the pages off to Dalton at midnight. This was the first exposure of his novel to his team, and Luke felt confident. He had cobbled together four chapters he thought were not all that bad to let the brass in on what they were paying for.

On the geriatric telephone a week earlier, Dalton had implored him not to send his absolute best stuff yet, convinced that wowing the publishers with a full, shiny first draft would hold more oomph in the long run. Luke complied, showcasing a sneak preview of the still-untitled novel that at the very least showed its true colors.

Luke went out into his yard before the 11:00 am conference call the next day, hoping a little physical work would juice up his energy levels. Mrs. Packard was thrilled to see her neighborhood crackpot back at his asylum-escapee antics, even making an effort to heat up some microwave popcorn to snack on while watching him dig a small hole, do nothing with it, and calmly walk back inside.

The ridiculous exercise worked like a charm. When the editor his publisher assigned him to collaborate with greeted him on the cranky old telephone, Luke was in high spirits. After cordial introductions, Anita Ravenwood dove into the business at hand with vigor.

"Super excited to be speaking with you, Luke," she said. "We read your pages, and I think a good place to start is a question we ask all of our debut novelists: *so what?*"

There was a long pause.

"I know it's an odd one to bring up right out of the gate, but at the heart of our work is figuring out why readers choose one book over another. With every novel that has ever been written available to consumers everywhere, why should I come to you? What's in it for me if I read a book by Luke Sullivan? *So what?*"

Luke cranked the timeworn telephone, silent.

"Let me ask a different question," she said. "How much of this is autobiographical?"

"A little of it, I guess."

"I'll need a very specific answer to this question, Mr. Sullivan," she continued. "If there are persons here who bear more than a casual likeness to real people, Legal should be on the case ASAP."

When dead air on his end was followed by Anita wondering if Luke's connection had gone down, Dalton reentered the conference call. Luke didn't say another word. He just stood there with his outmoded phone, feeling like a fuckup.

Twenty minutes later, the machine roared again, and Luke was there to pick up. Shaken, he said, "Should I be nervous?"

Dalton spoke with an amiable friendliness Luke wasn't sure was authentic or not.

"On behalf of both myself and your publisher, I want to reiterate that we're dedicated to considering and processing every challenge your process entails," Dalton said. "Take two is tomorrow. And let me go ahead and add that it would be helpful for me if you answered the questions posed to you."

"I froze," Luke said. "I'm sorry."

"No apologies necessary," Dalton said reassuringly. "It's all about the work. Greatness awaits!"

Luke wobbled at the idea of another conference call.

"We have two months," Dalton said. "Lots of time."

Luke didn't type a single word the rest of the afternoon. Crystal sent an email alerting him his reserved copy of *A Bend in the River* (one of her favorites, she added) was available. He did some research into the book's author, V.S. Naipaul, but mostly stared at the walls all day.

56

Unable to fall asleep, Luke decided to combat his insomnia with Henry James' *The Wings of the Dove*. Ten pages in, he felt the welcome tickle of boredom-induced drowsiness, only be woken by the recognizable double buzz of his smartphone receiving a text message at 2:00 am, which he figured was one of his buddies drunk-dialing him. It vibrated off and on again through the night, but Luke didn't care, having been thankfully lulled into peaceful slumber by James' prose.

While brewing coffee the next morning, he clicked on his awful little machine only to learn Nicole's father Miles had died. Luke got the details from Ray. Yana had gone out to the mall, and when she returned to their house in time to make a pizza dinner and watch national news, Miles was dead in the sitting room.

Luke knew Nicole was knee-deep in the administration that comes with funeral arrangements, so she probably wouldn't pick up a call, so after hanging up with Ray, he typed him a message with his giant, error-prone fingers: *Tell your wife I love her.*

He did a load of laundry, dusted off his black suit, and hoped against hope that B-Town would start. When she did, he began the drive back to Altoona.

Luke must have met Miles at Ray's and Nicole's wedding. The man was never much of a talker, but he was a movie buff, so he and Luke always had topics to discuss. He smiled as he crossed from West Virginia into Pennsylvania when he recalled the French Stewart made-for-TV comedy Miles insisted was the single greatest motion picture in the history of cinema. Luke had reservations about the validity of this, to say the least, but for all he knew, Miles might have been right: Luke certainly had never gotten around to seeing the damned thing.

They had gone gambling together once, too. Luke didn't roll dice on his own accord, but when he was with the Powells in Atlantic City, Nicole demanded everyone get out their pocketbooks: mama was gonna roll some bones.

And Nicole was *hot*. Luke only had to stand next to Ray and drink heavily as Nicole told him where to put his bets, quickly turning his hundred dollar investment into more than three times that. Luke remembered Miles, hesitant at the opposite end of the table, flashing a dopey smile whenever Nicole threw out a new derivation on "MAMA NEEDS A NEW PAIR OF____!" with decreasing sobriety.

When Miles jumped in, he did so quickly. He bet big and fast, and after six dice rolls from his daughter, Miles had amassed at least a thousand bucks in winnings. He refused to color up with the croupier, instead opting to carry his bulky chips across the casino to the cashier. Miles redeemed his money, and Luke saw him pull Nicole aside and hand her a wad of it.

She pummeled her dad with kisses and squeezes until he was beet-red with embarrassment.

If Luke were asked to tell a story at the funeral, that'd be the one.

Luke had a minute to catch up with Ray before the service, but Nicole was nowhere to be found, likely wrapped up in a hundred different preparatory activities.

He found a pew two rows behind the greater Powell clan, and the funeral began. A series of Bible readings were emotionally recited, then the stories came. Miles as a kid, Miles in the service, Miles as family man – even reticent Ray read a reverent paean to his father-in-law.

Nicole was last to speak, and whatever intermittent sniffles had already afflicted the room officially turned to out-and-out sobs as she gave a heartfelt speech recounting the volatile depths of daddy Miles' tough love that often prompted Nicole to pause with tremors of tears. She nearly succumbed to the emotion of the scene but held herself back.

When it was time, Nicole stood upright and with traffic-cop explicitness told the congregation to head to the cafeteria next door for food.

Luke stood near the door of the reception, hands in pockets, itching to get the hell out of town. He knew he'd be able to flex his excuse of a five-hour drive to legitimize a departure whenever he wanted, but he also didn't want to be the first to leave. Compounding this unease, Yana found Luke and gave him a cradling hug, unable to drum up the strength to say a word.

Ray brought over a plate of nachos, and he and Luke murmured to each other about the Eagles' terrible season. After their snack was gone, Luke told his best friend he had to go. As Ray hugged his buddy goodbye, Luke's chances for a clean escape were thwarted.

Vaguely familiar cousins and family friends crowded Nicole in the doorway. She shook their hands warmly, and they marched out into the Altoona sunshine.

Nicole twirled back toward the cafeteria and saw Luke. She kept up her steady veneer of matriarchal resolve for a minute, but once she was halfway to him, the collectedness she'd maintained all afternoon shifted.

When she threw her arms around Luke, she tapped into full breakdown mode. They embraced, right there next to Ray and the empty plate he wasn't in a rush to throw in the garbage, Nicole unloading a maelstrom of primal sobs that left remaining attendees awash in tears of their own.

Taking her time to pull away from Luke, Nicole wiped her nose on his shoulder and rubbed both her eyes before sarcastically adding, "Okay, *that* happened."

She rearranged herself, gave Luke a high-five, and shuffled back into social funeral mode. Ray was overwhelmed by what he'd seen, his tears dripping into nacho grease.

Two women standing a few feet to his left grasped themselves, one whispering to the other: "How does somebody not cry through that?"

57

In the back of his mind, Luke knew its demise was inevitable (if it hadn't already happened), so when Dweeb King officially hit the end of its road, it came as no surprise. He had abandoned the enterprise, after all, so the fact that a few months later business dried up with no grandiose fanfare made a sad sense.

What made him crazy, though, was that he did what he hardly ever did that morning: he answered his smartphone. When he saw an anonymous number pop up, he was worried it might be someone from Altoona calling about Toni, so he picked up, only to hear Matt Shelton's voice.

"Don't hang up," Shelton said. "It's Matt."

With classic disinterest in small talk, Shelton tediously explained how he'd attempted to Skype with Luke earlier in the day, but Luke never answered.

"Can't this wait until Friday?" Luke asked.

"We're shut down," Shelton said. "*Entertainment Talk* formally broke our contract last night, and all but two or three advertisers have jumped ship."

An anxiety rose in Luke, but he didn't want to exhibit even a shred of it to Shelton.

"We've been losing popularity for months."

"Since you took over, you mean?" Luke asked.

Shelton added, "We all get a little extra cash for our contract lapsing early. I'll get that check in the mail to you right away."

Luke threw the phone across the room. He paced for a while and checked his email, where a note from Dalton read: *Don't freak out.*

Anya came over that evening and cooked (using pans and ingredients she had to bring herself). She chose an adaptation of a Young Adult novel as the evening's DVD entertainment.

She fell asleep on the couch before the movie featuring talking pterodactyls and scantily-clad warrior women reached its finale. Luke didn't so much watch the TV as stare in its general direction, meditating on the death of the Dweeb.

The safety net beneath him had dissolved into dust.

Making matters worse, after coughing on a swig of wine, Luke got the hiccups, and was so nervous he'd wake Anya up with his loud fits he locked himself in the bathroom. He suffered with them for two hours.

Wiping his mouth with a towel at the end of the ordeal, he saw there was blood on his tongue.

58

The first words out of Pam's mouth when she arrived at the Charleston airport were: "Are you a pimp now?"

Luke sighed and picked up her bags. As he threw them into the back seat of the black Oldsmobile he had borrowed from Marion, he replied, "This is what you get when you refuse to ride in B-Town."

"That name is distasteful," she said.

Marion had sprayed heavy cologne in the sedan before Luke picked it up to cover his cigarette stench, which made the car smell like an oddly fruity ashtray. Pam complained about it as they sped toward the West Virginia mountains. Luke had planned a quick drive around Deer Meadow to show Pam the sights, but she was more concerned about what her hotel was like, nervous that if it weren't clean enough, they'd have to return to Charleston to find her suitable accommodations. The room Marion got Luke a sweet deal on at his nearby casino turned out to be thankfully up to snuff, and after getting herself settled, Pam had two desires for the late afternoon: getting a martini and meeting the girlfriend (in that order).

Pam, Donna, and Misty became fast friends. Luke's mom wasn't sold on Keene's lived-in white-trash decor at first, but once Luke perched her next to Donna and gave her a video poker primer, Pam was multitasking and gossiping with the Cougars of Keene's like a local.

"Tell me," Pam quietly said when she thought Luke wasn't paying attention. "What's the girlfriend like?"

"She's nice," Misty said. "Not great with the English, though."

Luke, absolutely hearing her, added, "I told you, mom. She's Romanian."

Pam took a sip of her martini and gestured Luke closer. "I need to whisper to you," she said.

"You *are* whispering, mother."

"Change your shirt," she said. "You have terrible B.O."

Rejecting this notion like an offended teenager, he replied, "You're crazy!"

Thankful to see Anya enter the restaurant, Luke walked over to her and kissed her on each cheek, opting not to enter into a full lip-lock in front of Mommie Dearest. Anya's attire was more formal than usual, and she gleamed with a straight-from-the-salon warmth. She extended a palm to Pam and said what she must have been rehearsing all day.

"Pleasure to meet you."

Pam took her hand. After too long of a pause, she asked, "What am I supposed to say? She doesn't speak English, right?"

Soon after this wayward introduction, Luke moved the theater of war from the video poker bar to what Misty assured them was Keene's nicest table. What followed was a meal banal in its lack of eventful occurrences. During an after-dinner drink, Luke found the confidence to put his arm around Anya, and happily let Pam recount old stories about Luke as a kid that she knew Anya wouldn't understand but told anyway.

"It was probably twenty years ago now," Pam started. "Grandpa Clark was still alive. He was even up and walking with his cane, if you can believe it. And before anyone was allowed to sit down for Thanksgiving dinner, he took you to the shed – the one with the fishing poles in it, not the one with all the tractor parts and machetes – and gave you a set of gardening gloves and a rake."

"He walked you to the front yard and pointed to a dead cat," Pam said. "A DEAD CAT! Just rotting there on the gravel driveway. Your Grandpa Clark was very much a cat person."

"You didn't get that gene," Luke said.

"Tell me about it," Pam replied. "He was insistent that if a cat died on the property, it was to be buried where it croaked. No one knew why. He had you pick it up with the rake and hold it a foot or two above the ground so he could dig a hole with a trowel right there on the spot. The miracle of Thanksgiving – you, your insane grandfather, and a cat carcass."

As Luke laughed at this anecdote, Pam noticed Anya not even pretending to pay attention. "I guess you had to be there," she said.

Luke squeezed Anya's hand, which directed her gaze back to the table. She stood up and headed to the ladies' room.

"I know you don't want to hear it," Pam said. "But you need to switch deodorants. You smell like butt. It's repulsive."

"Mom – cool it with the B.O. talk."

Misty walked by and asked how everything was. Pam rattled off a list of things she loved about her plain hamburger and side salad, pulling a credit card out of her purse (which got her double miles, she explained). Misty took off with it.

Pam then looked at Luke with a sudden melancholy. "You know what?" she asked. "This is the first real, adult, one-on-one conversation we've had."

"I was at your house a week ago, mother."

"Oh, when you come home, and your father's there, that's one thing. But I'm meeting your girlfriend. I'm seeing how you live, and *where* you live! We never did stuff like this when you lived in New York."

Luke sipped his drink. "Well, what do you think?"

Pam wrinkled her brow, giving Luke the impression she might start to cry. "You as a grown-up? It's strange for me. Fun, but strange."

59

44 BCE – 41 AD (according to Wikipedia)

I, CLAUDIUS,

ME#14

ROBERT
GRAVES
1934

GRAVES WAS ON RECORD late
in his life As saying he
hated I, Claudius — it
was only written for
financial reasons.

this probably
happens a lot

"I was thinking! 'So I'm Emperor. am!' What nonsense. !!"

60

Walking out of the bathroom, Luke recognized a sharp, steady pain inside his chest and panicked. After four rings, Roger picked up his phone.

"What?"

"It's Luke."

"Luke who?"

"From down the street."

"More chipmunk trouble?"

"I think I'm having a heart attack."

"That's not funny."

"I'm serious."

"Hang up and dial 911 immediately, then."

"Will you come pick me up?"

"Leave that to an ambulance. This is what health coverage is for."

Luke spared Roger his sob story about meaning to get insurance for months now but never getting around to it. "A quick ride to Urgent Care is all I need. Please."

"Jesus Jumping Murphy," Roger said. "Fine. But I'm not coming inside your disgusting rodent house. Be outside in five minutes."

Proof of how small Deer Meadow was: the administrative assistant working the counter at the Urgent Care in town was none other than Donna, Keene's resident video poker queen. She quietly shamed Luke when he explained he didn't have health insurance, but Roger jumped in and drove the conversation assuredly, knowing all the right questions to ask, showcasing a familiarity with the process that visibly impressed both Donna and the doctors who overheard him.

Luke had a terrifying self-realization in the examination room after a nurse took his temperature and told him to change into a gown. As he undressed, he looked in the large mirror hanging on the opposite side of the antiseptic chamber. His body had a different shape and curvature than it did last time he inspected himself. The man in the reflection was frail, sickly.

The doctor asked Luke whether or not he golfed. As Luke learned, once or twice a winter there was enough grass popping up above the snow to allow deeply committed swingers a good nine holes (in their snowshoes, of course). Doc assured Luke that he shot pretty well that morning, all things considered.

He set down his clipboard and gave Luke the once-over, checking his ears and shining a bright light in his eyes. When he prompted Luke to open his mouth, the doctor paused.

"Did you brush your teeth today, son?"

"Sure did."

"How many drinks did you have last night?"

Luke knew he was going to lie about this, but he didn't know how much he should cut back. The gray-haired doctor added, "At least three or four, I'm guessing. Your tongue is stained red with wine."

"Do you think that contributed to…?"

"Drinking excessively is never a good idea. Exercise restraint." The doctor flipped through his papers. "You're underweight by maybe ten pounds. You should reassess your diet. I bet this was a reaction to food."

"But it *hurt*," Luke said. "And heart attacks kind of run in my family."

"This wasn't a heart attack," he replied. "I can do a stress test, but I think that's unnecessary."

Luke sat nervously, fidgeting. The doctor added, "It's forty bucks if you want to keep the robe. Otherwise, you can change into your clothes now."

Roger asked for details on their drive back, but Luke didn't feel much like talking.

"It's odd he wouldn't prescribe medication," he said.

"I don't know what to tell you."

"What was your blood pressure? That must have had something to do with it."

"He said it was something I ate."

"You forced me to drag your ass to the hospital because you needed someone to burp you?"

Roger launched into an unhinged laughing fit. He was still wiping his eyes in painful amusement when Luke thanked him and walked out of his truck and up his stairs.

The sky above him had a very black look.

The familiar buzz of his chat program got Luke off the couch an hour later.

Ray: *Tell me something good. I've had a full rear thruster of a day.*

Luke: *I may have had a heart attack this morning. Went to the hospital and everything.*

Ray: *Bullshit. GFY.*

Luke: *It was scary, dude. I thought I was a goner.*

Ray: *Oh, please. You and I made a pledge in fourth grade that we'd die together as old men in a horrific roller-coaster accident. No fatal heart attacks for you!*

Luke: *Fair enough.*

61

Luke's Cornerstone experiment had reached terminal velocity.

He put Marc Lemaire's *Delinquent* (CS#431) in his Blu-ray player, sat back in his chair, and all but dared the film to blow his mind. And did it ever: it was a spellbinding stunner, a wondrously brief (seventy-six minutes!) snapshot of a tortured young soul locked in life on the fringes of 1950s Paris.

It stayed.

Other discs, lamentably, weren't so lucky. The majority of the pulpy samurai flicks Cornerstone was indubitably keen on releasing – *Samurai Uprising* (CS#301) and *Revenge!* (CS#331), for example – didn't hit their thirty-minute marks before they were earmarked for greener pastures.

The next two movies Luke prepared were gimmes, or at least he thought they were.

Time's Façade (CS#1) and Pascal Caron's *Playground* (CS#5) had unmistakable arthouse cred. The bleak wartime shadows lingering within *Façade* and the stark formalism of *Playground* prompted Luke to write Dweeb King reviews of their releases on DVD that were three times longer than they needed to be: he couldn't say enough about them.

But here in Deer Meadow, these films' buoyant sensibilities were sinking beneath the water line. Luke always had a sneaking suspicion Denis Fontaine was overrated – most international critics heralded his *Dutiful Ordinance* (CS#261) as one of the best films ever made in France, but he never understood why. And *Time's Façade* was outright boring.

Luke appreciated the bounty of its many virtues (Jacques Brunet with his slick haircut and perfectly-preened uniform, Fontaine's gentle direction of the film's strict-time plot development that evolves so neatly toward its climax), but never succumbed to its spell. The same fate befell *Playground*. Luke waited around for its final shot, that famous long zoom-out on the beach, but it didn't take Luke's breath away as it once did.

Luke let the movie's DVD menu loop on repeat as he puzzled over what had come to pass. He had been a paid professional in the trade, and in such a capacity, he could argue he was, therefore, a movie expert. He was no doctor of film studies, lecturing at conventions or writing academic books on astute intellectual subjects, but he had at least a little legitimacy in the field.

Had. Past tense.

There was the rub that was most painful at the moment. Luke was no longer a card-carrying film critic – he was a lowly consumer. Cornerstone Standard, the most esteemed studio in the business, recognized *Playground* and *Time's Façade* as major pieces of filmmaking, and Luke's puny discourses about how they were only *pretty great* were now patently inconsequential.

Luke looked back over a career he'd walked away from, poised at a juncture where the logical thing to do was mourn its passing and move on. He sat in front of *Playground's* DVD menu for an hour before falling asleep.

62

Daylin Hensley made out with Luke in his dream, and for some unnatural reason, he didn't like it. He repeatedly tried to pull away from her, but she kept her mouth on his, relentless. Complicating things, they shared this eerily long kiss in The Throne Room inventory space at The Cornerstone Standard offices, so even if Luke were able to escape from her advances, the space was so cramped with mountains of DVDs, he wouldn't have anywhere to go.

What Luke acknowledged right away as he sat up in his bed, glad to be awake, was the presence of his ghost. For the first time, he wasn't scared of it. The familiarity he now had with this shadow visitor had become a part of his Deer Meadow life, and as the goblin wheezed outside Luke's bedroom door, he found himself feeling not fear, but resentment.

Luke knew there was no actual demon waiting for him – this apparition had to be an invention, an unwanted theoretical zombie, one that would only return to the cosmos when Luke unlocked the secret code of its origins.

Was this phantom his moral counselor, sent from the outer limits to scare Luke shitless before teaching him the

true meaning of Christmas? Hell, if the wraith at his door
really wanted to inspire anxiety in Luke, it should take the
form of a health insurance premium or a statement of his
dwindling savings account balance.

And how pathetic was this? Luke could calmly address
issues involving a spirit from the netherworld who might
annihilate his soul, but what truly frightened him was money, the threat of bankruptcy, bills.

He'd never been depressed by the supernatural before.

63

He had logged six productive hours by the time he saw
a text from Marion demanding Luke stop by. Still feeling a
magnetic inspiration, Luke continued to type until the sun
vanished below the horizon. Pleased with himself, he picked
some wine out of his cabinet and headed Marion's way.

His Romanian friend refused to let Luke drink such a
beverage in his home. He gave the bottle to that wretched
girlfriend of his, leaving her and a host of other teetering
ladies in the kitchen as he walked toward his balcony.

Before joining Marion outside, Luke braved the storm
of the mobbed room, found Anya, and kissed her. For a
split second, the din of Romanian gossip stopped, and Luke
gave himself over to her. Anya smiled as she retired from
Luke's affections.

Marion lit a cigarette as Luke poured whiskey untidily
into his glass. "They are different, no?"

"Of course, thank goodness," Luke replied with slurring
approval. "But just because you have breasts doesn't mean
you can't write."

"It's not writing only. I imply this to all art."

"That makes you an asshole," Luke said.

"Think of the Louvre, the great museums in the world.
How many masterworks in there are painted by women?"

"I've never been," Luke said.

"You miss my point!"

"You want me to agree that men are better artists than
women."

"Yes."

"You're insane."

"If I were to ask you right now your five favorite writ-
ers, would you be able to answer me?"

"Probably."

Marion had a glint in his eye. He'd set a conversational
bear trap, and it was about to snap shut.

"Would any of those five be female?"

Luke considered mentioning Charlotte Brontë, but at
the moment he was drunk enough that he couldn't remember whether it was her or Jane Austen who wrote *Wuthering
Heights*.

Thankfully, he got a reprieve when the door opened and
Kristina hunchbacked her way onto the balcony. Shivering,
she whispered to Marion as he swept her onto his lap. A
yelp of playful pleasure escaped her lips, and after a ticklish
minute, she furrowed her way into the folds of his jacket.

Marion muttered something into her left ear that inspired a rainbow of emotions to flash upon Kristina's
crooked face. Appalled one minute, swooning the next,

slapping him gently on the shoulder after that – in awed drunken oblivion, Luke understood that Marion, a rampant, raging sexist, was playing this creature like a grand piano.

Marion gave her a kiss before shooing her away.

Luke asked, "How do you get her to respond like that?"

Marion grinned, instinctively knowing he had become Luke's sexual sensei.

"Right now, I am clothed," he said. "You are clothed. We hide from the world. We are men talking about ideas that mean nothing. In a bedroom, two lovers together – there we cannot hide. What I told Kristina now is nothing, bullshit. When we are nude side by side, when I am inside of her, when we are two pieces of flesh united as one, that is real. That is what matters."

Proud of his oratory, Marion returned to his cigarette.

In a spastic flash, on a topic that only he understood, Luke screamed, spilling his whiskey. "Emily Brontë! Emily Brontë wrote *Wuthering Heights.*"

64

"I didn't think I'd like them, but now I know," Misty said. "It's a better way of life."

It was almost closing time, and Misty poured one last round for Luke and the Keene's hangers-on who weren't quite ready to venture home. Luke recognized the thin woman from the post office talking to her video poker machine with her steep Boston accent as though she expected it to respond to her.

This had inspired Luke to try his own video poker game a while earlier. After his third glass of wine, Misty watched Luke put a twenty into the machine in front of him, only to be reinvigorated by their conversation, completely ignoring the game. Misty hoped he'd forget about it, which would turn his misguided poker investment into her biggest tip of the night.

"Don't you miss holding a book?" Luke asked as Misty poured herself a tequila shot.

"At first, maybe," she said. "But it's nice having my whole library in my pocket."

"Isn't it super small?"

Misty pulled out her smartphone, booted up the book she was reading, and showed it proudly to Luke. "I don't have to turn on a light in the bedroom if Pete has to wake up early. If I finish one book in a series and want to get the next one, all I have to do is hit a button. You don't have to drive to the store. It's cheap, too."

"I don't get it."

"Aren't you a big city hippie?" she asked. "How many innocent, helpless trees have had their lives spared by these e-things?"

In his mind, Luke concocted a sharply-worded retort to Misty's comment, one that addressed her point smartly. What Luke *actually* did was quite different: he took a clean napkin from a stack nearby, stuck his tongue all the way out and vigorously scrubbed it, thinking such an act was something he could accomplish without drawing attention to himself.

The entire establishment watched in flabbergasted silence.

Finally finished with his grotesque demonstration, Luke
nonchalantly wadded the napkin up and tossed it in (well,
toward) a garbage can to his left.

As though the last ten seconds hadn't happened, he
calmly began making his point. "It's interesting," Luke said.
"Because when it comes to e-commerce…"

Misty signaled an immediate full-stop. "WHAT," she
screamed, "did you just do?"

65

The napkin-tongue story got a lot of mileage at Misty's
annual *Fuck You, Valentine's Day* barbecue. Anya tugged at
Luke's arm as they first entered the bartender's home, evidently wanting an explanation as to why every person in the
place had paper towels in their mouths upon their arrival.

Lucky for Luke, three of Anya's Romanian pals inter-
cepted her before he could invent some cockamamie rationale to the event, which he only half remembered. And
hell, she wouldn't have understood him anyway.

Grabbing an icy beer from a cooler, Luke went out to
Misty's backyard and choked when he looked up: in the sky,
sinister clouds careened ferociously. There was a tinge of
inky blue still visible way off to the east, but the rest of the
nightmare above him had been overtaken by weather that
seemed darker than it had any right to be. It was straight out
of a science-fiction film.

Misty's husband tended to the three barbecues in operation and talked to a pair of coworkers from his construction crew. Pete was a bulky, welcoming fellow, a silver fox with a long, rocker's haircut. He introduced Luke to his equally burly drinking buddies, and Luke asked the group about what the hell was going on in the West Virginia sky.

After a moment of shared apathy, one of them said, "She comes once a year, within a hundred miles or so."

Pete gestured to Luke with his spatula. "The twister, man! Today could be the day!"

Deciding he had to go indoors before he started asking which of these strangers had an underground shelter he could escape to, Luke walked past the beer coolers to the expansive spread of food that fanned out across Misty's kitchen counter. There were wings and fried nuggets of minimal dietary value, slaws and pies, sauces and breaded treats.

Maybe it was time to try the local cuisine.

Halfway through his second pass, he couldn't believe what he'd been missing out on all these months. Luke loaded another plate of hush puppies and watched the skies through Misty's kitchen window, worried about his cabin suffering tornado damage.

The hideous irony of the party was that it prompted Luke to have the two most productive days of his Deer Meadow stint. As he'd later recall with intestinal confidence, less than a minute into Misty's annual reading of the *Fuck You, Valentine's Day* manifesto (imagine *The Night Before Christmas* only with references to the Cougars of Keene's instead of Santa), Luke got what Dalton had referred to in college as *the gurgle*.

Needing to go to the bathroom is a daily element of the human condition, Dalton argued, but sometimes digestion is not a reliably fluid activity. Every so often, a trigger might snap somewhere between your *in* point and your *out* point, and expulsion urgency would increase exponentially, often inducing a sound from deep within your gut: *the gurgle.*

Luke experienced this twenty minutes after his triple-helping of greasy food.

Misty's house wasn't particularly large, and while there was a commode available for partygoers, Luke didn't want to be the guy who upended the celebration's only pit stop, destroying both the room and anyone within five miles of his blast radius.

Without alerting anyone, Luke ducked out the back door, hopped Misty's fence, and trotted home at the fastest pace he could muster without jostling the unclean fireworks inside him.

The sky was a treacherous gray, full of such beautiful natural discord families were out on their lawns, staring up at the apocalyptic display. After passing the grade school half a mile from his cabin, Luke's *gurgle* worries spiked, and he understood his obituary would cite him as being that former mid-level TV personality who shat on some Deer Meadow family's lawn during a Valentine's Day twister.

Yet thanks to a cyclone-inspired miracle, this did not come to pass. Sweating profusely and thankfully solitary, Luke locked his front door behind him and spent the next 48 hours never more than twenty feet away from the can. He set up his laptop on the bathroom sink and typed twenty-five pages over the weekend.

66

All Cornerstone anguish aside, the writing was pouring out of him. Luke had no Dweeb King conference calls to dread, no extraneous diversions pulling him out of the whirling vortex of his work. He didn't even shower or pace through his usual coffee routine one day, drawn to his computer by an idea that ballooned into a block of manuscript Luke felt oddly confident about.

After breaking out of what he could only describe as a spell, he had completed nine pages, a quantity that was a good day's work in itself, and it wasn't yet 10:00 am. He enjoyed his belated first cuppa, feeling both satisfied and driven to keep up the rhythm.

By mid-afternoon, there was very little gas in Luke's tank. He tried digging a hole around 2:00 pm, hoping it would recharge the animation he'd channeled during his morning hours. Mrs. Packard across the way was particularly charmed by his footwear. Her neighbor dug a hole in the snow while wearing flip-flops and white tube socks. She was confident the police were going to call her in for questioning any day now.

Luke jumped right back into it after his outdoor chore, but thought it might be time to put the workday to an end when he read over a line of dialogue he'd given to Daylin Hensley: *Oh my God, that is so, like, bad.*

It was part of the process to compose stink bombs like this before using the delete button liberally, but he was maxed out. Luke stood up, stretched, and reached for his coffee mug.

What occurred next can only fully be understood by

those who know what it is to be genuinely, categorically spastic. To err is human and all that, but there is a level of anti-coordination saved for the deeply inept, a tendency within certain individuals for operatic displays of dumbassery. For such poor souls, on a relatively regular basis, synapses misfire in stupendous glory.

Luke had a perfect, impeccably absurd example of this. Back at Pedersen High, he and his girlfriend Ashley were once driving to a coffee house not far from school, Ashley talking a mean streak as Luke pulled into the establishment's parking lot. Without warning, Ashley pointed at two mutual friends of theirs crossing the lot in front of them.

She yelled, "It's Greg and Amy! Honk!"

It was best, Luke added as an aside whenever he'd share this story, to imagine it happening in slow-motion.

Picture Ashley's words leaving her mouth, entering the airspace between the two of them, and finding their way down Luke's ear canal en route to the sector of his brain that analyzed language. After processing these sounds, his brain would send appropriate signals, and his body would act accordingly.

Science, right?

As it happened, Luke's reply to Ashley's innocuous statement was to take both hands off the steering wheel and clap three times. Ashley laughed so vigorously at this misdirected demonstration that she peed her pants a little.

Keep this anecdote in mind as we return to Deer Meadow (go ahead and keep it in slow-mo). Here was Luke, reaching for his mug, gently lifting it, and in a critical second completely and hopelessly forgetting how a human being held a coffee cup.

The liquid fell in one graceless splash onto the laptop's keyboard before the mug hit the computer, the desk, and

176

Luke's chair on its inglorious arc to the floor.

The rest of the afternoon was spent tracking down someone who could offer Luke a prescription for this setback that didn't involve a two-hour drive to a tech shop that might or might not be able to do anything about it. He found advice claiming a period of drying-out would undo most problems caused by a liquid spill.

After cracking the laptop open *exactly* the way some techie dork documented in an online video, Luke stepped back from his coffee-stained travesty and needed to not be in a room with a goddamned computer any longer.

Anya was working, he knew, and Marion didn't pick up his phone. Infuriated that the greatest writing he'd done in Deer Meadow was now a caffeinated garble of zeros and ones, Luke decided to warm up with a shower and head down to Keene's for a few.

Freshly steamed, Luke brushed his teeth, ran a comb through his hair, and walked to grab a t-shirt and some boxer shorts that had finished their spin in the dryer. He opened the machine, found a white shirt among the platties, and proceeded to put it on.

What Luke didn't know was that this task was about to tailspin into yet another bout of spazzy thrashing that would rival the Ashley car horn incident and his coffee computer splatter as one of the most blundering moments of his life.

Luke, bare-ass save for the shirt he was attempting to put on, flailed about. In a defiantly unerotic modern dance, Luke fought emphatically with the garment, his business blubbering about, his torso engaged in a life-and-death struggle to, you know, put his hands through the armholes of a shirt.

And the profanity – if Luke were able to replicate on the printed page the vividly descriptive, hideously vulgar epithets that fell out of his mouth like purses being emptied, he could cement his literary legend. This nitwit, grappling to conquer a t-shirt in a drag-out gladiator grudge match, found tears welling in his eyes. Amid the sounds of tearing fabric, Luke took the fucking thing off and threw it on the ground, panting and spent.

Knowing full well no blame could be placed on anyone but himself for what had transpired, Luke closed his eyes and smoldered as he made the realization:

It was not a t-shirt. It was a pillowcase.

The bullfight was over.

To add insult to injury, not only had Misty taken the day off, but Jeremy said to Luke while pouring him a second glass of wine, "Dude, you might want to change your shirt. You smell a little ripe."

67

To his immense relief, Luke's coffee-bathed computer booted tentatively back to life after a two-day dry-out, and he celebrated the occasion by having Anya over for dinner and a movie. When they greeted each other, he noted she'd brought two bags: one full of food, the other carrying toiletries and a change of clothes.

Even with the day's encouraging technical news and the promise of sex lingering in the room, Luke tuned out the world around him, preoccupied (again) with The Cornerstone Standard.

As the cheerleading dance-off in Anya's movie began, Luke considered the more famous moments from Sam Brisco's *The Big Tent* (CS#369) that he'd watched over his lunch break. Here he was in that same old frustrated purgatory, recognizing the value of this cherished old film and complaining about his complicated view of it.

This Cornerstone business was driving Luke bonkers. What was he learning? Who gave a shit if some dude in the woods loved or hated a foreign-language movie most Americans had never heard of? Didn't it all come down to taste anyway?

Before another interminable inner soliloquy began, he called bullshit on himself, as Dalton would say. Luke was sipping wine next to a beautiful woman, and bellyaching that *The Big Tent* was a pretty damned well-made movie.

Luke was *angry* because movies were *great*.

He laughed loudly enough that Anya shushed him (though Luke wondered what kind of nuanced dialogue she might have missed). Recalling a classic overconfident moment, he zipped back to 2009, where a Dweeb King contact had arranged for Luke to attend a screening of J.R. Greenwood's reboot of *Intergalactica* in NYC.

Seeing as he shared a partiality to all things sci-fi, Luke brought Dalton along, and they geeked out over a nice dinner beforehand, reveling in a discussion of the more essential facets of the *Intergalactica* universe, like the visible antimatter Lieutenant Anthony discovered in *Intergalactica IV: Multiverse Mixup* (*Outrageous!*, Dalton exclaimed).

Dalton had fun with Greenwood's *Intergalactica*, finding it fun and action-packed, but contemptuous Luke had a different take. What had been so endearing to him about the show and those first films from the 1970s and 80s was that their grandiose concepts were unmistakably more important than any artistic craftsmanship or, to be sure, believable acting. These movies were lovable not in spite of their inconsistencies and errata, but as a result of them.

For Luke, J.R.'s shiny sports car *Intergalactica* was shamefully sleek, regrettably accessible to everyone. There weren't any oblique, unfathomable improbabilities within it.

Where, indeed, was its visible antimatter?

Thought-provoking sci-fi once ghettoized in appeal only to fringe-dwelling dorks had now been given mass-market approval. This new *Intergalactica* wasn't a franchise only nerdy blockheads like Luke consumed – the football squad, cheerleaders, *and* dweebs could all enjoy it together, and that, to Luke, was blasphemy.

Luke finished his sermon at a bar after the screening, loudly stating: "I hated it. It wasn't shitty enough."

"Pause?" asked Anya, running to the restroom.

Taking a swig of wine, Luke understood he'd spent enough time agonizing over Cornerstone and J.R. Greenwood's *Intergalactica* for the night. When Anya returned, she prompted her beau to restart her DVD by kissing him.

Luke became mesmerized at how terrible Anya's movie was. There was absolutely no way Cornerstone would ever release an edition of it, which was a relief.

He couldn't sleep. Luke watched the way light from the moon hit the ceiling above him for a while, listening to Anya snore peacefully at his side, wearing one of his old rock concert t-shirts. He lingered in this slipstream for a while, then popped out of bed.

Anya found him in his office the next morning, wearing only his boxer shorts, typing furiously.

68

Of all the folks in Luke's Deer Meadow circles, the only one who showed marginal interest in his Cornerstone exercise was Roger. It surprised Luke that the old man would consider such an affected concept, but when Roger had him over to help move some boxes, Luke leafed through a sizable wasteland of his VHS tapes. Here were westerns, WWII movies, multiple copies of rusty actioners.

There was one title out of place.

"*The Lonely Lady*?" Luke asked. "I never would have pegged you as a Sweetie Blanchard fan."

"Check the tape on that one."

Luke shimmied the cassette out of its case and discovered *The Lonely Lady*'s true identity: a skin flick so naughty and sleazy Luke didn't dare read its title out loud.

"Sometimes you need a little help, you know?" Roger explained.

As Luke hauled packages of newspapers and magazines to shelves in a closet down the hall, he said, "You have pretty strong taste in movies, Rog. Most folks don't bother with titles more than a year old."

"Most people are assholes."

Luke opened a beer and waded out into Cornerstone territory. "I bet you even watch movies more than once."

"I have to," Roger said. "You Hollywood peckerheads haven't made anything worth seeing in a theater in decades."

"What was the last good one you saw?"

Roger thought for a second and popped a beer of his own. "*Bullet Beach*, maybe?"

"That one's fifty years old!"

"Who cares?"

Luke picked up a Sunday paper, as he often did, and took his time devouring it. Saving the Arts and Book Review sections for last, Luke stoked the fire — extra cold outside, more snow coming — and scanned a story describing a new play he didn't know anything about opening off-Broadway in a week.

He opened to the section's second and third pages and settled with a fright upon what might as well have been an obituary. Crammed onto a dense page of ads and movie times was a face Luke recognized immediately.

Matt Shelton.

Dweeb King Dethroned was the snippet's headline. Luke was innately curious as to whether his name was mentioned in the *Times*, but he couldn't focus on the article's text.

Kisser looked thin, manicured, less frumpish than usual.

Luke threw the paper in the fire, refusing to have it in his house any longer.

He expected Dalton to call any minute.

69

He knew men were often guilty of overestimating their erotic talents, but Luke suspected he had electrified Anya the night before. As though the waning winter air triggered a beast in him, while she was making dinner, nature in its rawest form took over. Barely finding the wherewithal to turn the stove off, Luke picked her up and carried her downstairs.

She sighed when Luke dropped her onto the bed, but this frivolity quickly transformed into a desperate fervor. She threw her head back and buckled with his weight upon her as he caressed her thigh and made his way up her side, her arms tightly wound with his.

As Luke pulled Anya's shirt up, he took carnal gratification in recognizing her breathing had changed. She showcased a complete loss of sensory control, unable to exercise any authority over the way she was responding to him.

Her head bobbed as he unbuttoned her jeans. Her moans became erratic and unhinged, gasps for air followed by scratches of pale coos. Clothes, lips, hair, breath – on top of Luke's perfectly-made bed (they had no time to deal with sheets), he lifted himself above her and looked down at her heaving chest, glimpsing a flutter of gooseflesh coarse from her breasts down to her bellybutton.

Luke had never seen anything like it.

It distracted him for a full calendar day. He went through the motions of checking out a new round of ML100 titles from the Deer Meadow library and discussed with Crystal the highlights and distractions he'd found in Paul Bowles' *The Sheltering Sky*, which he'd finished earlier. He tried starting another ML100 novel, but even lost within the library's dusty stacks, he couldn't stay focused.

Marion was right. Bedroom connections were the real deal.

70

"Of course they are! Marion knows."

The Romanian took a final gulp off his bottle of beer and threw it over his balcony's guard rail. He and Luke stared at each other for a moment, wondering if it had perhaps evaporated in the night air, then laughed as it crashed into the dumpster below. Marion wasted no time using his lighter to pop open another.

When they saw that Marion's landlord had moved the apartment building's dumpster into tossing distance from the Romanian's balcony, they decided to keep their whiskey sealed, opting instead to blast through a case of beer. With childish desires to break shit, the two idiots snickered with destructive glee as they threw their empties into the night, their better halves busy inside watching television.

By their fourth round, the conversation had veered from film and art toward sex. Telling Marion about the other night with Anya, Luke gave as little detail as he could, trying to deduce whether there had been any word around town as far as his prowess was concerned (Marion hadn't heard anything).

Marion lit a cigarette. "We're drunk, right?"

Luke coughed loudly. After he was certain he hadn't inspired a round of the hiccups, he returned his focus to the Romanian.

"You're in show business," Marion said. "Ever done gay stuff?"

Luke cleared his throat. "You know, I haven't," he said. "Folks say it's great, but I never had a ton of interest. You?"

"One time."

"Yeah?"

"There were things I liked about it," he said with a shrug. "What can I say? I love to orgasm."

Luke carefully asked, "Was it serious with this guy?"

"A queer friend of mine from Croatia walked me through the motions, that's all."

"Sounds clinical."

"I wanted to know, and he didn't mind teaching me." Marion took a long drag off his cigarette. "Women smell better."

"How far did you get with this Croatian dude?"

"All the ways."

"No shit?"

"I did everything to him; he did the same to me."

Luke reddened. "Now I understand why you hug people the way you do," he said.

Luke tossed his last empty into the dumpster, and after it crashed, he stuttered, "I wonder what happened to her."

"Use the computer. Look her up," Marion said. "She was good-looking?"

"I don't remember," Luke said. "This was summer camp twenty-five years ago. She had big cans. I can tell you that much."

"Excellent."

"What were summers like in Romania?"

Marion's eyes were barely open. "Poland," he said. "Born in Romania, childhood in Poland."

Luke nodded as Marion began humming to himself. "I haven't thought about Poland in a long time," he said.

A car passed, crossing from left to right in front of them. As its sound faded, Marion made a clicking sound with his tongue, and his eyes welled with tears.

"Alexander," he said, unable to fully form the words. "We had a dog named Alexander."

Marion wept. Giving him an opportunity to howl for a while, Luke reached out and placed a hand on Marion's shoulder. For a while, neither man said a word.

Luke saw Toothpaste in the sky above him, clear as day. *Ride the lightning*, he thought.

71

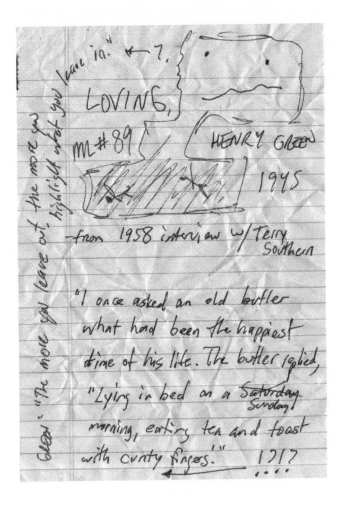

LOVING,

m #89

HENRY GREEN

1945

from 1958 interview w/ Terry Southern

"I once asked an old butler what had been the happiest time of his life. The butler replied, "Lying in bed on a ~~Saturday~~ Sunday morning, eating tea and toast with cunty fingers.'" 1717 ....

GREEN: "The more you leave out, the more you highlight what you leave in."

72

Luke hadn't planned on going to his college buddy Keith's wedding, but when the guy finally got him on the telephone, regaled him with some choice off-color P.F. lyrics for old times, and rejected Luke's *Will Not Attend* RSVP, Luke caved and bought a plane ticket. He wouldn't have much time to explore Chicago, but it was a chance to get away for a day.

Marion agreed to take him to the airport, though getting the Romanian up in time to catch his 8:30 am flight out of Charleston was an ordeal that Luke vowed not to undertake a second time. He made sure he packed notepads for the journey in case the muse tracked him down, but once in the air, Luke instead downed complimentary cocktails and did the crossword puzzle in the paper.

The wedding was enjoyable, the bride beamed, and the party was a riot. Luke fooled himself into thinking he could step away from the shenanigans at 10:00 pm in an attempt to be functional enough to catch his 7:45 am flight the next day, but Blotto abandoned this self-imposed deadline.

He got chummy with a bridesmaid, Magda, a talkative woman in her late forties. She was proudly Polish, and when Luke told her his girlfriend was Romanian, Magda changed the subject, not taking all that kindly to anything from the region (Marion hadn't let Luke in on this national rivalry). Blotto danced with Magda and her entourage long into the night, singing repugnant Piss Flap songs with Tommy and Keith like they were film school losers again.

As the after-midnight episode of the wedding party kicked off, Blotto knew that with air travel imminent, if he didn't slow down, Operation: Barf on the Plane would be a *go*. Telling Magda this, she sat Blotto down and presented him a free and clear way to avoid such an outcome.

"Are you a wine drinker?" Magda asked.

Blotto would never lie about this. "All the time," he said.

"Then take this good Polish advice. It will leave you clear-headed for your trip home. Merlot is best. Sip your Merlot slowly."

This made sense to Blotto.

"When you finish your glass, take a shot of tequila and down it straight away. No chaser, no salt. Then return to wine. You'll thank me."

Blotto vomited ten minutes after trying this, wishing he never mentioned his girlfriend's Romanian descent to Magda. Having what felt like no liquid or food in his body, Luke barely made it to the airport three hours later.

He wasn't much of a plane-sleeper, but having been decimated by Magda's evil Polish genius, his riddled body was able to get in a couple of snoozes on the trip back. He overheard a flight attendant tell a woman sitting in front of him that there was always a little turbulence over Indiana, so it came as no surprise when a string of shakes hit the aircraft a few minutes later. After some minor chop, the plane settled back down, and Luke wandered again toward sleep.

Without warning, the plane rocked, split off its axis by what seemed like thirty degrees. Its right wing punched up into the sky, and for a brief second, the entire craft was helplessly unstable. A man Luke couldn't see screamed.

Somebody must have thrown up, too – that undesired

yet obvious aroma came floating through the plane.

The pilot came on the intercom and joked, "Who put all those potholes up here?"

No one laughed.

Luke suddenly realized that a miracle had occurred. Once the fright of the moment subsided, he felt no dull wine-tequila-wine pain. Thanks to this near-death experience, his hangover had been shocked into submission.

He got out a notepad and wrote during the rest of the flight about Daylin Hensley and the mean-spirited Polish lawyer cross-examining her on the stand.

73

He fell into a clean, manageable pattern. Luke would write in the morning, jog in the forest over lunch break, research all afternoon, and either swing over to Anya's, drunk-philosophize with Marion, or pester the Cougars of Keene's after sundown.

Mostly, though, the writer was writing.

He wanted to check the weather forecast and had no idea where his smartphone was. He hadn't used it in a week. Digging through his office desk drawer, Luke located it and plugged it in.

Having been burned by Shelton when it came to unknown numbers, he typed one that had tried him repeatedly over the last several days into an internet search and saw its source was a hospital in Kentucky.

A throaty nurse answered when Luke called, but she couldn't help him – no one who shared his last name was in the facility. He hung up and checked voicemail. There was a message from Ray about a horror miniseries that was way better than it should have been and some zero-import Dweeb King press queries, but nothing from a hospital.

The smartphone buzzed an hour later, and Luke saw the same 502 area code from earlier. Excited to get to the bottom of this mystery, he used his business voice: "This is Luke."

"I've been calling your ass for three days!" Roger said. "Can you pick me up from the airport tomorrow?"

"I can get to Charleston tomorrow, yeah."

"No, the Deer Meadow airport over by the post office," Roger said. "8:00 am."

The line went dead.

–––

Luke got to the airport early and was glad he did. Populating this tiny airstrip and the single-building terminal next to it were wonderfully odd characters Luke wrote about on the notepad he'd brought with him.

There was a waitress with neck tattoos in a bright yellow dress and a white apron who poured him a cup of watery coffee in a Styrofoam cup. In the lobby, an obese janitor took his sweet time arranging macramé plant holders. And best of all, a bald gentleman named Nez with a quarter-inch gap between his front teeth (much wider than Luke's) sold cigarettes and generic candy in a small booth.

Nez told Luke he could take his coffee outside and sit on one of the benches while waiting for his flight. Luke did so, and after a few moments, he heard a helicopter. He didn't spot it until a full minute later, when the chopper appeared above the ridge beyond the airstrip, its volume tripling from a whisper to a roar. Pummeling the air around it in sweeping jets, it touched down on the paved strip, its rotors slowing ever so slightly as a ramp extended out its side door.

Uniformed men dashed around and exited the helicopter in reverse, pushing a familiar geezer in a wheelchair. One of them flanked Luke with a clipboard, asking who he was, and upon hearing the right name, pointed for Luke to sign a piece of important-looking paper.

Before he knew it, the airmen had reloaded back into the chopper, and the dragonfly was in the air again, retreating toward the hills it had crested earlier.

As Roger came closer, Luke held onto a welcoming smile, but something was off. Luke first considered how long it had been since he'd seen him (*Two weeks, maybe?*, he thought), but whatever time had passed, the old man wheeling up to him was not the Roger he remembered.

His mop of white hair was intact, and the way he tried to hide a sullen smirk was classic Roger, but this person had deep spots on his forehead, and eyes so surrounded with dark flesh it seemed as though they'd sunken back in his head. Twenty pounds of the guy were missing, as well, the flesh on his arms sagging with stretchy bounce.

Roger wasn't in the mood to talk, refusing to answer any questions Luke had for him. Even "You want me to stop off and get beers?" didn't elicit a response, which made Luke nervous. Roger wasn't tethered to the wheelchair – he stood and folded the device before shoving it into B-Town's back hatch – but once they arrived at his house, Luke plainly noticed he was not getting around the way he once did.

Luke finally found an inquiry Roger might respond to.

"How did you get to ride in that bitchin' helicopter?"

"Army vet health benefits," Roger said. "For some commie government reason, they'd rather chopper me out to a hospital in Louisville than have me take an ambulance to a nearer place. My tax dollars hard at work."

"I gotta tell you," Luke said, attempting a joke. "I think your doctors botched your sex change surgery."

Roger grinned as he walked from the office into his bedroom. "Just ticker trouble," he said. "Went for new prescriptions at my doctor's office and I flunked a test."

Roger grabbed a bathrobe and entered the bathroom, closing the door behind him. Luke had already asked him whether there were family members he should alert as to his condition, and he felt like bringing this up again but didn't act fast enough. Roger turned on the faucet, and Luke heard him fiddle with a washcloth.

"Wanna see something cool?" Roger asked.

"You can keep your saggy old man balls to yourself."

"Cool it, sailor. I kept my undies on," Roger said. "Come on."

Luke pushed the door open. Roger was seated on the rim of his bathtub, his robe open, revealing the man underneath. He explained how his doctors took a vein out of his thigh – there was a deep gash at the bottom of his powder-blue boxer shorts – and replaced a clogged artery in his chest with it.

"I'm in the zipper club!"

Roger reached for help standing, and as Luke pulled him up, his eyes focused on his sternum, which was a mangled collection of stitches, bolts, and skin.

Not offering Roger a warning, Luke started to cry.

He nestled his face into Roger's shoulder and had one of those embarrassing outbursts that was more snot and noise than tear-shedding. This act increased in loudness when Luke sensed Roger patting him on the back.

Roger tried to separate them by asking if seeing the old man in his underwear gave Luke a boner, but Luke was sobbing too loudly to hear him.

74

After months of listening to his client extol the charms of West Virginia, Dalton figured at the very least it would get Luke to shut the hell up about it if he came out and saw the damned place. But aside from enjoying the Romanian lady candy swirling around Anya's apartment, Dalton found the bucolic boredom of rural life too dull to stand. He invented a last-minute meeting he had to attend in the city the next morning so he could leave as soon as the sun rose.

Luke knew all was not well when Dalton shanked Keene's due to Misty's meager Scotch selection. And while Dalton wanted to see the ridiculous phone that had been installed in Luke's place, he showcased little desire to linger in his client's dusty abode. He did, however, comment on the dog-eared copy of Robert Penn Warren's *All the King's Men* on Luke's desk, noting it was one of his favorites.

Dalton was more comfortable in his hotel suite at the casino outside town. He played the role of razzle-dazzle agent expertly once he and Luke arrived there, and after flashing twenty dollar tips to select well-connected employees, Dalton had bought a bathing suit for Luke, some

Gluten-free snacks (his new thing), and a barely-acceptable bottle of Scotch that would be added at exorbitant cost to his bill.

The two of them hit the hot tubs on the hotel's roof and were the only ones there. Steam created a thin layer of mist that hovered in the air. They sat, drinking, slowly kicking their feet in the bubbling water.

Dalton said, "Tonight is the first night I've seen you kiss a woman."

"That can't be."

"I've been on double dates with you, and you've brought girls to Super Bowl parties and all that, but I've never observed a Luke smooch."

"I told you it was exciting here!"

"So, this Anya," he said. "Is she the real deal?"

It was a question that had been swimming laps in Luke's brain for months, but hearing someone else pose it to him set off depth charges. Familiar enough with the way Luke worked, Dalton knew the inquiry had sent his sensitive buddy into shut-down mode.

Dalton finished his Scotch, lied about being tired, and insisted his night had reached its end. As he exited the elevator on his hotel room's floor, he patted Luke once on the back.

"To be continued," he said before flip-flopping down the hall.

75

Luke thought a quickie Altoona homecoming would recharge him before the drudgery of his final six weeks of writing presented itself. B-Town got a flat tire two hours out of Deer Meadow, which was a pain in the ass, but a lack of drama at the Sullivan house was pleasantly refreshing.

Pam didn't mention Luke's body odor once.

He didn't spend much time at Ray and Nicole's, seeing as their mutual pal Larry from high school was throwing a big party that Saturday. Luke helped a very pregnant Nicole transport marshmallow treats and freshly-made cookies from their kitchen into ice chests and ultimately onto buffet tables at Larry's with as little bruising as possible.

Larry had a ranch-style home with a swimming pool and a manicured lawn that spanned an acre of flat land. Luke greeted fellow Pedersen alums vaguely recognizable from old yearbooks, struck up statistical conversations with the guys from his fantasy football league, and drummed up passable enthusiasm every time Lori came over to show off a new design face-painted on her cheek.

Mostly, though, Luke found himself gripped in an antisocial state, only finding solace in the uncomplicated act of drinking beer while soaking his feet in the pool.

On this bright Pennsylvania afternoon, Luke wondered what his high school buddies might think about Anya. Would she fit in at all? He knew he had forged a connection with his European lover, but couldn't imagine folding that aspect of the Deer Meadow world into his Altoona lifestyle.

This probably meant he was treating her like a jerk.

More pressing than this navel-gazing narcissism was the

fact that here he was, not writing. Splashing quietly, Luke lamented having come home. He was thrilled to see his favorite faces, but he shouldn't have been there.

Lori joined Luke, plopping her feet in the water next to his, a rainbow unicorn new to her upper right cheek. There was an easy silence between them.

"You'd call yourself a happy person, wouldn't you?"

"Yeah," Lori said.

"How do you keep from overthinking things?"

Luke truly expected the precocious child to respond to his question, but her splashes stopped as her attention turned to Larry's roaming housecat, Reba, who was currently on the approach. Lori squealed as the nonplussed feline rubbed up against Luke's back.

Nicole somehow saw this from the kitchen and yelled, "Don't touch! You're allergic!"

Stymied by this parental admonition, Lori stood up and donned a look of mock disappointment. On a dime, her expression changed again, this time to one of shock. She grabbed Luke's arm with one hand and pointed at Reba with the other.

"Uncle Luke!" she exclaimed. "That cat just had an IDEA!"

As if this had been a nothing statement, Lori swapped moods again and ran inside, leaving Luke neutron-bomb dumbfounded. There was dopey adorable-kid kitsch in what had transpired, he'd gladly concede, but that barely dulled the edge of the fact that Luke knew he'd just heard the single most interesting sentence ever spoken in the English language.

He, the "professional" writer (*Make those air quotes bold, boys*, he thought), had spent months agonizing over a novel that had been trumped by a child's aside.

Smarting with jealousy alone at the pool, Luke felt like garbage.

Back in Deer Meadow, he printed THAT CAT JUST HAD AN IDEA on an index card and tacked it on the wall behind his computer. Like a haunting sutra, in his last weeks in town, Luke often found himself sipping coffee and staring at the words, sometimes for hours at a time.

76

He popped a load of laundry into the dryer before heading over to Roger's. Luke was *this close* to nailing down a title for his book, and he figured some manual labor would help bring a moniker into focus.

As he took a roundabout route to the old man's place, Luke considered his front-runners – *What Lies in the Dark, Contemplation,* and *Kentucky Mist* were close, but not right. He hopped up the stairs and rapped on Roger's screen door before barging in with an amiable swagger.

There he was, sitting quietly in his corner chair, his new walker at his left, a price tag still tied to its curved handle.

"I met my new nurse yesterday," Roger said. "I hate her."

Luke gave the Roger what he hoped was a considerate

glance.

"How 'bout you come in three times a week?" Roger said. "I'll pay you! There will always be beer around. The lady who shops for me could set it up."

"Why don't you ask *her* to be your nurse?"

"I'm serious."

"No, you're not," Luke said, changing the subject. "Do you want me to vacuum, or should I just bring some firewood in?"

Before he got a chance to answer, Roger made a face.

"Did you step in shit on the way over here?" he asked.

The dryer finished its cycle with a beep. Luke was excited to switch out his jeans, damp from the snowy walk back from Roger's, for flannel pajama pants. Deciding to change his shirt, too, he took it off and smelled it.

Had he stepped in shit?

Lifting the shirt again to his nose, he recoiled. Humiliated that all this time his armpits had truly been toxic offenders, he sniffed both the collar and the bottom seam of the shirt and found them to be equally foul.

He picked out a shirt from the dryer, and it too stunk of rotten ass. Luke emptied the machine and triple-checked every lint trap and accessory he could adjust, but nothing explained the odor he now understood was infused into all clothing he owned.

Revealing strands of lint and dust, Luke pulled the dryer out of its chamber as far as it would go, the silver duct connecting it to the wall at full tautness. He turned it counterclockwise, and the hose fell loose to the floor.

Luke noted that on the dryer-side connection to the

duct, there was a bushel of built-up lint. Scowling, he set three big handfuls of the stuff in a pile behind him. He took a rag and a bottle of window cleaner and proceeded to wipe down the rear of the appliance, making sure there was nothing left there that might cause a stench. Luke took the air connector in his hand and attempted to reattach it to the machine.

It was heavy with something.

Bunched inside, jamming the air duct, were chipmunks. Deep-fried chipmunks.

These poor suckers, no doubt stoked at having discovered a warm nook to wait out winter, had crawled into the dryer output hose to nest, only to be burned alive by the exhaust of the machine.

Luke donned a set of dish gloves from the kitchen upstairs and excavated chipmunk carcasses out of the dryer hose, nearly filling one of his outdoor garbage cans with the rodents in the process. Luke cleaned the mudroom from head to toe and took a long, thorough shower.

Knowing he'd have to incinerate his wardrobe, later that night, he ordered new clothes online in his birthday suit, opting to pay to have them all delivered the next day.

77

Luke read *Heart of Darkness* for an English assignment and was the only person in his high school class who gave a shit about it. Part of this general disdain was its timing – few kids warmed to a book that had to be read over summer break – but Conrad's fable stuck with Luke.

Currently revisiting the novel, Luke found himself more smitten with it than ever. He had been worried it would feel well-worn but not mandatory, a sense so many of his Cornerstone DVDs were inspiring, but Luke invented excuses throughout the day to abandon his work and read Conrad's novel instead.

He finished it and stared into the forest, considering not only *Heart of Darkness*, its characters, and their dubious fates, but whether that senior year English teacher of his was still around.

- -

Luke had been so taken with his journey into *Heart of Darkness* that he wanted to talk about it.

Actually, he just wanted to talk.

As Anya served the lasagna she'd prepared later that night, Luke realized he hadn't said a word out loud the entire day, and as they settled into their assigned seats on the couch, Luke resisted turning on the TV.

"Let's practice some English!" Luke said.

Battling an impulse to steal the remote from him, Anya mumbled, "Movie is better."

That was that. The TV set hummed on. Anya blew him an air kiss as the first of many previews began to play.

78

"No way," Anita said on the telephone. "No extensions."

Luke was biting his nails and sweating. He had instigated the process of submitting full chapters to his editor, which had initially appeased Anita, but as he was discovering, with each new round came a freshly complicated barrage of industry mumbo-jumbo and ever-intensifying deadline reminders.

"We will cite you in breach of contract if we have to," Anita said.

"It won't come to that," Dalton added.

Dalton and Anita bantered back and forth about the novel not coming in at anything longer than 300 pages.

Anita shuffled papers. "So let's confirm," she said. "Four weeks from today you deliver us a final manuscript, ready to be edited."

For some reason, Luke took on a Southern drawl. "You bet."

"We're done here, then," Anita said. She hung up.

Dalton kicked into a pep talk. "One month! You got this!"

"Yeah," Luke said. "Here's hoping."

With a surfer's calm, Dalton asked, "What are you up to

tonight?"

"Well, I'm going to finish this movie, and…"

Dalton cut him off squarely. "Nope," he said. "You're writing tonight."

Luke did what his agent suggested, even preempting his evening session by digging a hole in the backyard, one that Mrs. Packard, looking from her kitchen, noted was his deepest to date.

Twenty minutes into writing Daylin's lawyer's closing trial arguments, Luke got the hiccups. Swearing and screaming in pain, they dissipated after an hour, but the convulsions exhausted him so fully he had no choice but to turn in early.

79

He wrestled writer's block all morning, but at some point, while staring at THAT CAT JUST HAD AN IDEA, Luke felt a fracture, the tectonics within his head rearranging into a new landscape. For a stint, Luke couldn't type fast enough. He'd look up at his computer screen and see damning streaks of autocorrect red, but grammar and spell-check had to wait.

Luke hardly noticed that Deer Meadow found itself under the spell of an aggressive spring snow. Blinders up to everything but the work before him, Luke pummeled through concept after concept. They appeared out of no-where, both fully-formed and adjustable, able to slide into whatever setup Luke saw fit.

There was a faint sense of personal catharsis in this for Luke. The writer in him was concocting altogether fictional narratives, but whenever opportune, he'd hijack a nugget from his own life to lend a detail an organic singularity. This collision of fantasy and selective recognizance allowed him, every now and again, to catch a hurried glimpse of his own soul.

Luke found himself channeling a character named Neil Lynch, an army vet and newly-elected judge, who was a stodgy, unlovable oak tree of a man. As grating as he needed the guy to be, Luke wanted to insert a tidbit of peaceful quiet into his character's genome, a recall that might smooth out his more villainous instincts. His fingers stopped dancing for a moment, and he considered what from his life and times he could commandeer to the honorable Judge Lynch.

Luke hadn't thought of Woody Silva in thirty years.

The two boys became fast friends in Mrs. Adams' third-grade class at Baker Elementary in Altoona when Woody enrolled halfway through the fall quarter and was assigned a seat next to Luke.

Woody and Luke found commonality in matchbox cars. The alliance of Woody's outstandingly complete collection and Luke's proclivity to invent audacious narratives for them involving aliens and cyborgs pinned against each other in four-wheel duels to the death made it easy for the boys to be left in a room to entertain themselves for hours on end.

Luke recalled a Friday snow day when his parents had to work. Phil, the brother closest in age to Luke, had left for college that August, so there were no free Sullivan babysitters in the house to tend to the runt. On a lark, Luke recommended to Pam he go to Woody's, where his new buddy's stay-at-home mom would absolutely be around.

Most matchbox car campaigns with Woody involved an hour of play that would have to end unfinished because of homework or some other lame chore, but on that glorious winter morning, the two boys found themselves with all day to goof off.

Luke even managed to cajole Pam to agree to a sleep-over, so he and Woody were presented with the only opportunity they ever had in the span of their friendship to prepare and execute matchbox car battles from dawn to dusk.

When Woody's mom came in to signal lights-out, Woody was already asleep in a chair, and Luke was lying on the floor, defiantly holding onto his waking self, mumbling orders about calling giant fire trucks into action, toys grasped tightly in his palms.

After being softly awakened, Luke got into his sleeping bag and closed his eyes, hearing Woody's mom pick up his pal and place him on his bed.

In his Deer Meadow kitchen, Luke could still hear the way Woody Silva's voice sounded when he said to his mother, "I want to sleep on the floor next to Luke."

If life had handed Luke a different set of particulars, this could have served as a sweetly delicate homo revelation, but that wasn't the case here. In this fleeting snapshot of a rapidly disappearing youth, Luke simply felt essential, valued, and, he supposed, loved.

As the boys evolved through grade school and Luke paid more attention to *Saturday Night Live* than school sports, their interactions all but completely dissipated, but here, at the tender fabric of Luke's human experience was a cherished, warm-hearted Woody Silva.

And now it belonged to Judge Lynch.

It was over. Ended.

80

RAGTIME ⎡ – call Nana
⎣ – bday present for Loki (not a book!)

ML #86   E.L. DOCTOROW
                    1975

"It is never right to play
    ragtime fast." – Scott Joplin,
from the quote that opens the book

– both fictional characters and
real people here – Houdini, JP Morgan

RAGTIME – supposedly a
                contraction of
                "ragged" and "time"
Doctorow died in 2015

His 2005 book THE MARCH is
supposed to be great – ask Crystal!

81

Dalton said he'd help Luke out when he heard the news, but Luke didn't need a car, especially with his deadline approaching. And if he were to return to NYC after his voyage to Deer Meadow came to an end, a new vehicle wouldn't be worth the investment. Also, Roger wasn't using his truck much these days, so Luke had wheels if he needed them.

This didn't make B-Town's demise any less heartbreaking.

It was just another afternoon. Luke had received an email from Crystal that some ML100 novels had come in for him at the library, so he got in B-Town and turned the ignition.

Silence.

Luke had Donna convince her husband to drive out and check if there was something minor that could revive B-Town back to even barely-functioning life, but after looking, Avery had nothing to offer but condolences.

Luke searched online and discovered to his surprise that he could sell the Cherokee for more than he expected, even if she wasn't running. This high in the mountains, there were always buyers on the market for a four-wheel-drive SUV or its parts.

He rejected this idea. The thought of walking around Deer Meadow and seeing someone else driving B-Town was not an option. Also, as anyone who ever met B-Town knew, it was likely that the SUV would burst into flames at any moment (she surely was overdue), and Luke didn't want that kind of blood on his hands.

He tracked down a salvage company. If he left keys under his door mat, this outfit would replace them with a check for $200 and tow the car away right then and there. With a heavy heart, Luke set up a time for B-Town to shuffle off to vehicle Valhalla.

Stupefying the snooping Mrs. Packard next door with new and inventive oddity, Luke looked imbecilic as he set up his small tripod on the steps of his cabin in an attempt to get one last snapshot of him and his trusty partner in crime.

Between not knowing how to use his camera's timer and having issues getting the tripod to cooperate, Mrs. Packard got a full fifteen minutes of enjoyment watching her neighbor take a picture of his car (for who knew what sort of perverted reason).

Luke patted B-Town's hood lovingly and scanned the camera for keepers as he walked inside, officially beginning the wait for the salvage company executioners.

He couldn't bear it. Luke wanted to be on site to stage one last operatic farewell to the girl, to celebrate her launch into the big parking lot in the sky, but the image of B-Town being rolled out of sight made his stomach tighten.

He picked up his copy of *The Grapes of Wrath* and headed for the woods.

82

He drove Roger's truck to the library and returned *Native Son* and *Lolita* with a woebegone dismay, realizing there was only one novel left in his ML100 odyssey. Luke spoke with Crystal about the last stone in his path, Anthony Powell's *A Dance to the Music of Time.*

When Crystal did her initial search for the novel in the library's system, nothing showed up.

This began a bookworm tango that acted as a fitting finale for Luke's months-long task. Their first clue into the riddle of Powell's book was that it was no garden-variety tome: *A Dance to the Music of Time* was a twelve-volume compilation published between 1951 and 1975.

Luke's internet research gave him the impression the works were hot commodities in the UK, but the magnum opus never caught fire in the States.

Working with Crystal to track down Powell's dozen books was a nerdy thrill, but a fog of hysteria hovered within Luke's mind at the consideration he might have to leave his project 99% finished. Breaking his *No E-book* edict, Luke enlisted Crystal to help him unearth an electronic version – he'd read it on Misty's phone if he had to, dammit – but none were available. He price-checked some online retailers, too, but except for some highly-valued collectible printings, none were in stock.

Thankfully, Crystal was able to shake down one of her colleagues in Connecticut who had access to paperbacks of the Powell books, and she offered to sell them to Luke for $100.

The box arrived on his doorstep a week later, and Luke put off all the writing and editing he had on his docket, dedicating himself to finishing his ML100 game, tearing into Powell's first installment with rabid eagerness.

He made it a hundred pages before he started skimming.

A Dance to the Music of Time was probably an accurate

and properly-detailed representation of coming of age in mid-century England, but to Luke, it was prim and proper baloney that involved a lot of tea drinking and fussing about.

After spending the weekend slogging through all twelve parts, Luke donated the books to the Deer Meadow Library, happy to see them go.

83

Luke was genuinely pleased when the ghost who had haunted him through the winter came back for one final spook. Anya quietly sleeping next to him, Luke considered growing a pair and meeting the specter face to face. He wished the idea of proving his virility in front of his girlfriend made him want to more actively pursue the visitor, but macho wasn't exactly Luke's strong suit in times of peril.

Luke's mind took him back to his New York college days, where he and Ashley Hogan ate at a Mexican place not far from his dorm. The two of them had enjoyed a frisky afternoon of lovemaking before heading to La Barca, a seedy dive that offered free chips and a burrito the size of your head for ten dollars plus tip.

They bought margaritas and looked passionately at one another between sloppy salsa dips in the booth at the rear of the restaurant they liked so much. This dreamy exchange of theirs was upended, however, as Ashley's baby blue eyes were drawn to Luke's left.

He turned to see a substantial cockroach on the seat a foot away from him.

Ashley was nonchalant, calmly suggesting he smash it, but Luke took a wildly less masculine approach, moving next to Ashley on her side of the booth. He turned his head toward the first La Barca employee who acknowledged him, whispering in the whiniest voice he could muster, "Um, waitress…?"

They laughed about this pantywaist display of Luke's for the rest of the evening, it having all but negated any bedroom prowess he had established during daylight hours.

Luke opened his eyes and sat up, ready to man up and face his apparition once and for all.

That being the case, he didn't want the phantasm to see his wiener, so Luke spent five minutes trying to reach the boxer shorts on his dresser without either waking Anya or exposing his precious bathing suit area to his resident poltergeist.

Two things happened when Luke walked up the stairs. The second was that Luke switched on the living room light, exposed nothing out of the ordinary, and went back to bed. Before this, though, Luke saw someone.

If he stared directly at the mirage, it became television snow, but if he kept his eyes from focusing, he could make out somebody sitting on his couch, giant eyeglasses reflecting dimming fireplace embers.

It was The Dragonslayer. It had to be.

This was no demon. It was seventeen-year-old Luke sporting his Ethnic Vest, white tube socks, and sandals.

Luke almost looked in The Dragonslayer's direction for a minute and resolutely kicked that light on, rendering his adolescent self invisible.

84

Roger sent Luke to the grocery store to buy hot dogs and snacks for an annual poker game he hosted for some of his army buddies. When Luke returned, he didn't enter the house right away, staying out of Roger's range of vision for a minute, quietly watching the guy attempt to get around in his new walker.

Luke got the barbecue ready and greeted David and Mark, the first wave of guests, who were what Luke imagined folks in Deer Meadow might be like before he spent any time there: rugged farmers with penchants for chewing tobacco and moonshine.

Tad, who Luke would soon learn worked for Marion at the casino, entered next, pushing Simon, a jokester wearing a light-up plastic visor, into the house in a wheelchair from the garage.

David and Mark were far more interested in cards than they were in back-fence talk, but Tad and Simon were chatterboxes, and once they started, they didn't let up.

Toward the end of a seven card stud hand that was taking forever to deal because Tad was racking his brain trying to remember names of girls they met on shore leave during the war, Simon asked Luke to tell the group something about himself.

"Don't answer any question the writer asks," Roger said.

Tad asked, "A writer, huh? What have you written that we'd know?"

Roger guffawed.

"Some of my movie reviews were read by millions of people."

"Yeah, on the internet," Roger added.

"Doesn't count," Mark said.

Tad made his case: "Internet's only good for porno movies and weather reports."

"I made a decent living working online," Luke said.

Tad stared at Luke seriously. "You ever bang a chick in front of a camera?" he asked.

"Not that I can recall," Luke said.

"I hear that pays well. And hey – there are worse jobs."

Roger showed the gang his winning hand and moved the chips on the table closer to him.

He looked to Tad and said, "Like anybody could rub one out watching your limp dick tickle at some lady."

"Can you imagine?" Mark asked. "If I was in my twenties, I could show up on a Monday morning, go through business with eight or nine girls before quitting time, and just golf the rest of the week."

"What about people seeing your ass?" Simon asked. "Wouldn't that would be embarrassing?"

"If a naked woman is getting railed on the left side of your screen, and my hairy buttcrack is thrusting up and down on the right, guess which one you're going to be focused on?"

The guys laughed. Mark even smiled, the only time Luke saw him do so.

"Yeah," Mark said, "That's what I'd do if I were a young man again. Or – what's it called when a woman takes off her panties, and you go in and take all the hair out?"

Luke asked, "A bikini waxer?"

Mark pointed, nodding. "I'd do that well."

Tad bounced back into Luke's original topic as Simon dealt a hand. "You made money out there on the computer, huh?" he asked.

"How much an hour, give or take?" Mark asked.

"That's the trade-off," Luke said. "You get to make your own hours, which is great, but you're working pretty much all the time."

"The year I retired I made sixty-five dollars an hour and was contractually obligated to leave the office by 5:30 pm," Tad offered, checking his cards. "You do anything close to that?"

Luke figured if he broke down an hourly rate during his Dweeb King days, it would be unequivocally south of minimum wage.

"Maybe it's time for you to find a new line of work," Simon said.

85

Luke wanted Aldo Bruno's theme from *45 Lies* (CS#3) to be played at his funeral. From the dandelion shower at the beginning of the film, gorgeously alerting the Tuscan mountain town central to the film that spring was coming, through episodes featuring bawdy prostitutes with giant breasts and tree-trunk thighs, *45 Lies* wasn't just a classic film for Luke. Every time he put it on, it was as if he were revisiting a country he'd loved at first sight.

After the swell of Bruno's finale, the TV went dark. Luke looked to the shelf beside it. What had been a broad compilation of CS films, a collection Luke had painstakingly curated over the years, had been reduced from nearly five hundred titles down to forty-five.

The ones that didn't make the cut needed to be dealt with, now that Luke's experiment had come to an end. The prudent thing to do, Luke knew, was to take the discs to a used record store and cash them out. He'd make some money, and the recycled movies would find their way to DVD shelves in budding film lovers' dorm rooms – it was a responsible way to hand down the Cornerstone tradition.

Yet here was Luke's B-Town gene twitching into action again. For decades now, these spinning movie discs held an esoteric value to him. He couldn't shake the vision of a weasely hipster in skinny jeans buying *his* Hedlund movies, putting *his* discs in a non-calibrated DVD player and peeking up at *Winter With Mary* (CS#123) or *Sunburst* (CS#641) when he wasn't texting or checking his social media profile page.

No, Luke thought. *Never.*

A second insane epiphany arose within Luke. During his months in Deer Meadow, he had dug at least twenty-five holes in the backyard. He could arrange ten or twenty Cornerstone discs in each hole, cover them up, and that would be that.

Acting alone, he'd never have to explain his ridiculous logic to anyone, and no unqualified consumers would have access to his previously-adored treasures. If Kevin Turney himself called him out on it, Luke might have to do some creative explaining, but when would that opportunity ever present itself?

You see, thought CS chatroom contributor Gus Van Cant, *they have nowhere else to go.*

He waited until after 1:30 am to begin. It was fucking freezing. Luke dug in the moonlight, and over the course of two truly polar hours, his cover-up was complete.

Mrs. Packard didn't watch Luke from her kitchen window. She'd never know.

86

He had a feeling there'd be a lot of Anya in the character of Daylin Hensley. Whatever went on inside his girlfriend's mind was a secret known only to those fluent in Romanian, but in physicality, upon leafing through the nearly-completed first draft of his novel, Luke was surprised and even a little proud to see that Daylin and Anya were reflections of each other.

Luke had printed out his manuscript and spent the day making minor changes to it. It was too long, but he'd find sequences to cut. There was unquestionably work yet to be done, but the plot wasn't a mess, the twist at the ending appeared to fit, and there throughout was Daylin.

The novel acted as a view into an alternate world for Luke. In this still-untitled book of his, there was no language barrier between him and Anya. It was a non-issue. Having melded straight-up fiction, tendrils of personal memories, and details stolen from sources far and wide, Daylin Hensley was a composed, unique, familiar identity.

Was Daylin Hensley a more well-rounded human in his life than Anya? What he had with his Romanian companion seemed to be working (somehow), but was theirs a mutually beneficial vague abstraction, or were they dancing toward love?

He imagined Marion telling him Anya wanted to get married, that she was ready to commit to a life with Luke. What would his reaction be to this? She'd have to learn English, seeing as that was the only major wrench in what was otherwise a free-flowing partnership.

Or maybe not. Could they share decades together without engaging one another in conversation? Maybe it was Luke who needed to learn Romanian.

If he were poised with a choice between being with Anya and not being with her, he'd surely choose the former. Whether this meant he loved her or not, he wasn't sure.

Luke wished there were more Cornerstone movies or ML100 titles to investigate. He craved distraction, a chance to put his brain on pause for a minute. He stared at the forest outside, the moon shining through its trees.

Had he seen his last snow in Deer Meadow?

87

—got Women in Love from Crystal — it's, this books sequel. Yippee!

THE RAINBOW, connection?

ML#48   D.H. LAWRENCE
                                    1915

DIPSHIT HONKY?
DICKHEAD HOOTENANNY?
DINGLEBERRY HYPNOTIST

This was banned?

LUKE SULLIVAN   LICKS SULLIVAN

Really?

BRAINBOW!

"If I were the moon, I know where I would fall down."

↑ what the crap does this even mean?

88

Luke and his buddies from high school addressed the topic of visiting former teachers of theirs during the holidays when they were all back in Altoona, but they never made good on it. But after being revitalized by his novel's surprising progress, Luke got a bee in his bonnet to track down his English teacher Ms. Linton, to tell her all about his ML100 trek.

Ms. Linton picked up her phone and spoke with a hoarseness that had become deeper and more discordant in the twenty years since Luke last saw her. He attempted some polite small talk, learning she was always at home and that afternoons were best if he felt like stopping by.

After making pit stops at his parents' place and the Powells', he headed toward Ms. Linton's home way out in the boondocks, recalling how much she loved *Portrait of the Artist as a Young Man*.

Toward the end of spring semester, she had dangled a fascinating quandary to Luke's class. If any of them could guess in a short essay why Stephen Dedalus was her favorite literary character of all time, she'd be very pleased (there was maybe a restaurant gift card in the deal, too).

If any of her students hit the nail on the head, no one heard about it. On the last day of school, when asked if anyone unlocked the Dedalus code, she smiled and said, "Have a great summer," before letting them out twenty minutes early.

Luke knocked on Ms. Linton's front door. When it opened, the frail, bony lady holding a cigarette and propping herself up on her walker said after a minute, "You don't look the same, either."

Ms. Linton adjusted the black wig on her head and
shuffled slowly back into the house, leaving the door open
for Luke to follow. He nervously started in with menial
chatter about how wonderful it was to see her and how long
it had been since they'd caught up, but she didn't engage
with him on any of it.

As she made her way to her orthopedic recliner, Luke
continued his harangue about missed alumni reunions,
where his classmates were today, and what Ms. Linton had
done since retiring, at some point not being able to ignore
the Home Shopping Network playing on a TV in the center
of the room.

She lit a fresh cigarette, deciding after a long while to
turn from the space-age juicer on the monitor to her former
student.

"I saw you on the TV," she said.

"What did you think?"

"Can't remember. You married?"

"I'm not."

"Kids?"

"Nope," he said. "Did you ever have...?"

He didn't finish. Ms. Linton raised her hand, exerting
that disciplinary prowess Luke recalled being scared of in
her classroom. She gave him a blank stare like he was the
last customer in her checkout line before break time.

"You know," she said, "you're the first from that fucking class of yours who bothered to come see Patty."

Petrified at her use of profanity, Luke replied, "What
about Ashley Hogan? You guys were close."

"I heard she sent me an email, but I don't do that."

Luke had a speech planned, one that would bring up
James Joyce and his recent reminder of *Heart of Darkness'*

literary wonders, but Ms. Linton stopped that idea flat in its tracks.

Through the cigarette smoke, Luke thought he saw a crack in the ice when she asked, "Well, what have you done with yourself? You were on the TV, but you're not anymore. You're not married. You're not a father. What are you?"

"I've written a book," Luke said.

"Where can I buy it?"

"I submit the manuscript in a few weeks."

Ms. Linton unleashed a fiery cackle. "You haven't *written* a book. You're *writing* a book."

This stagnant send-off (*It was a send-off, wasn't it?*, he thought) impelled Luke to start lifting himself off the couch.

"I did want you to know something," Ms. Linton said, softer now. "I try to mention this to all my students who come visit."

"You were kids, and kids don't know any better, but for what it's worth, I remember you all. Amy Wolfe, Gregory Houser, Ashley Hogan – I could list off every student in yours and every other class I taught in my thirty years at that school."

Luke steadied himself a little, sensing Ms. Linton was getting ready to pay him a compliment.

"You either thought I couldn't hear or didn't notice." She took a drag. "It's neither here nor there, but you must remember I was a big girl. Fine."

"But when you consider those high school glory days of yours that you've already tried to get me to smile about, know that while I was trying my best to educate you little fuckers, you were terrible to me."

"It wasn't all the time. Most of you could be okay. But each of you had a mean streak. *Fatty Patty*. I heard that a hundred times. You, Luke Sullivan, even called me that in my own classroom."

Luke didn't know whether to storm out or beg Ms. Linton's forgiveness. She decided for him, turning back to the TV.

"Anyway, just FYI," she said. "Have a nice life. You don't have to come back."

89

Breathing fire, Luke wondered how much prison time he'd have to serve if he murdered his editor in cold blood. In a calmer state, he might begrudgingly concede he and Anita were making strident headway together, but the act of fine-tuning his initial draft into a finished book was a draining burden.

Their early calls were helpful and illuminating. They established that Luke was the macro and Anita the micro in this process. Luke had eyes on the grand picture of the novel as a whole, while Anita's expertise was with the syntax and grammar of the book's basic construction.

With Anita holding the reigns, every paragraph, phrase, and syllable was scraped over with microscopic consideration. In fact, it was one of these unending discussions about semi-colons that was presently making Luke so irate.

But Anita knew how to manipulate Luke like a puppet on a string.

Each day, Luke would frazzle with snooty negativity

after they'd spent hours steeped within the minutiae of his prose. Anita's tactic at this juncture would be to implore they move on to another chapter, promising Luke they'd come back to their current trouble section later.

He'd agree reluctantly, and Anita would guide the pair onto a new segment that needed ironing out. A day or two later, Anita would ask Luke to reread what they'd worked on, and the knee-jerk disquiet he originally felt was all but washed away.

No doubt about it: she was improving the material.

This was Anita and Luke interacting on a good day. Today, however, Luke was leaning over his desk, screaming, "You can take your past participle, frankly, and shove it!"

Luke had been trapped on this call all morning, having agreed to wake up early so Anita could break away in time to catch the noon meeting or meal or cult ritual or whatever the shit it was that was so important to get to.

"We have to stay productive, Luke," Anita said. "That we're so passionate means these are battles worth fighting."

He had to keep reminding himself she was making the book better, and a better book meant more press, and more press meant more sales – it added up. Yet Luke wouldn't give up the point at hand, electing to read two slightly different versions of the same paragraph on his computer screen for the fortieth time.

Anita said, "If you came into town, we'd get through this in a week."

Dalton had advocated for this, as well, but Luke the technology dinosaur wouldn't bite.

He reached the end of his tolerance for the events at hand. "Fine, let's go with yours," Luke said.

"Great," she replied happily. "Early one again tomorrow. 6:00 am."

Luke set his coffee on the table. It was time to switch to something stronger.

Every Romanian in town was at Keene's. Anya rushed up to Luke and gave him a quick peck on the cheek. Marion, three sheets to the wind, screamed Luke's name and walked his way with open arms. As though Luke was letting a dog hump his leg for a minute just to get it over with, he allowed Marion be as embraceably demonstrative as he wanted to be.

This one was a doozy, too: Marion pulled his entire person against his friend, and littered Luke's face with kisses. Truth be told, Luke got more action from Marion than from Anya that evening.

Marion turned to Misty. "I need two whiskeys!"

The Romanian threw his arm around Luke. "We're here to celebrate," he said.

"Good," Luke said. "I've had a shitty-ass day and could use some cheering up."

Misty handed a pair of shots toward the men. Luke and Marion clinked their glasses and downed the swill.

"A dream has come true for Lobo!"

Marion stepped back inelegantly and put his thumbs and forefingers together, establishing a movie shot. Luke just stared at him. Marion then hollered to the crowd in Romanian. The restaurant went wild, responding with a racket. He clumsily sat back on his barstool.

"We make wedding videos in Romania!" he said. "It's time to go back, anyway. Work is no good here with the season ending. My father knows a man who has equipment. It is arranged."

A pinprick tapped at Luke's gut.

"Some will stay, the ones with rich boyfriends, you know. The rest of us – why not travel together?"

Luke knew what he'd feel if he caught Anya's eye, so he kept his gaze firmly on Marion, who, even this drunk, was quick to regard how sad Luke's face had become.

Holding him close, Marion said, "Don't be so sour! You're leaving soon, as well, no?"

90

Packing wasn't going to involve a tremendous amount of elbow grease on Luke's part, but he was nevertheless disinterested in it from the get-go. Sure, he knew he wouldn't live in West Virginia forever, but he had grown used to Deer Meadow's distinctive idiosyncrasies and wasn't prepared to let them go.

During his last week in town, his only major duty was to slaughter through sessions with Anita in the morning, so he had most of the day free to ramble. The snow had stopped falling, and while there wasn't yet that green lushness to the trees that dwarfed him so mightily (Roger said it'd be there in a month), there was a sense in those dense thickets that they had endured the rigors of winter, and were ready for the heat and humidity their xylem and phloem innately knew would return.

Then there was Anya. Their parting was imminent now, not a distant eventuality: the end was here. Roger, Marion, Misty, too – these mainstays would in seven days transform from fixtures of Luke's daily life to warmly-recalled shades that may or may not figure into his future.

If exploiting every moment left in town meant that much to Luke, he could rush over to Misty's house to get some last-minute face time with her and the Cougars of Keene's. He could pull double shifts helping Roger make his home as wheelchair-accessible as it would soon need to be. He could even fuck his girlfriend like there was no tomorrow.

But here was Luke doing what he did best: wasting time.

He poured a glass of wine and came to terms with the fact he'd lost his taste for the cheap-swill vino he was inclined to purchase in bulk. That being said, a laser-focused drive to drink came roaring in a flash as he waded through the day's entertainment news.

Gus Van Cant trolled the Cornerstone forums as he always did, and he almost didn't recognize Matt Shelton's oafish face in a browser sidebar. He clicked with haste.

There was Kisser, boisterously happy and well-dressed, trimmed and fit. As Luke learned, Shelton had been named president at a new publicity firm out in California. According to the article, with his decades of experience with Dweeb King, he was an obvious choice for a start-up that was going to reinvent the way consumers accessed home entertainment in the digital world.

This in itself didn't break Luke's heart, but the next paragraph sure did.

The bigger photo of Shelton, as it turned out, was a zoom-in. The full press conference picture had Shelton standing to the left of all the other founding members of Dweeb King.

These guys – *My guys*, Luke kept thinking – were dapper and poised, big smiles one and all.

Clyde, Evan, Koji: the Dweebs looked great without him.

Dalton called on the oldy-foldy telephone about ten minutes later. It was the only time in his stint in Deer Meadow Luke disobeyed his agent's rule and didn't pick up.

91

Luke's parents hated surprise parties, demanding at least once during family gatherings that if ever one was staged, the culprit would be judged and shamed. Luke's brother Brice, however, decided it was time to defy this long-standing rule.

Sullivan get-togethers over the holidays were rare, with in-law commitments and kiddo event schedules complicating even casual reunions. It was impossible to get all Sullivans in the same room at the same time between September and January.

But April had just begun, and Luke's brothers and their kin found a window for everyone to descend on Altoona *en masse*. And there was news: Phil and his wife were expecting their fourth.

Brice, on a telephone call Luke spent two weeks not returning, knew there'd be a brunt of animosity from Pam and Kyle at first to a surprise invasion, but their grandparent reflexes would kick in, and the closest the Sullivans ever got to recreating the happy-go-lucky family dynamic of a Norman Rockwell painting would begin.

As though she was being mugged on the street, when Brice jumped out from behind the front door to scare Pam, she screamed bloody murder. Kyle was agitated, as well, ecstatic to hug and kiss grandbabies, but reminding each of his sons that surprises were punishable offenses.

The shock waves died away, and Kyle and Pam were thrilled to hear about Phil's new arrival (a girl, finally). And not having a formal holiday hanging over the party inspired an easygoing fun that kept the event remarkably relaxing.

There were no gifts to exchange, no large-scale missions to plan and execute, no itineraries to keep. The Sullivans ate like kings, threw back a few, slept it off, and planned a big breakfast together before retreating to their respective corners of the world.

Luke was too preoccupied to be fully engaged, remaining hampered by the cold Deer Meadow darkness that followed him around. He found momentary respites in impromptu kickball games with his nephews, but familial interaction only distracted his nail-biting consternation for minutes at a time.

He had a sneaking suspicion that as an older man he'd look back and wish he'd participated in occasions like this one more actively, but this didn't keep Luke from spending most of his Saturday staring into space.

The Sullivan entourage wasn't slated to head to the airport until mid-afternoon the next day, but Luke knew he needed to get back to West Virginia sooner rather than later. He chatted and cajoled with Toni, who'd arrived early in the morning with her new full-time caregiver, tried to find an answer in regards to his weight loss that would appease inquisitive sisters-in-law, and peeked through smartphones congested with kid photos.

Luke waited for his mom to head into the kitchen so he could stage a quick private goodbye, but Pam's grandma avalanche was in such a free-for-all it took her an hour to even get up for a coffee refill.

Luke tapped her arm lightly and lied. "Ma, I gotta go," he said.

"You tell Misty I read that book she recommended, but couldn't get into it."

Brice's wife Emily entered, dirty bowls in her hands. "Misty?" she asked. "New girlfriend?"

Luke hugged both women and jingled his keys before heading out the back door.

"Nah," he said. "Just somebody I used to know."

92

THE DEATH OF THE HEART

ML #84 ELIZABETH BOWEN

"As for Thomas, the longer
he lived, the less he
cared for the world."

"Pity the selfishness of
lovers: it is brief,
a forlorn hope; it is
impossible."

93

"I don't want to," Donna said.

Winter had officially left Deer Meadow. Every window in Keene's was open, and the April air breezed through the restaurant, ruffling the pages Luke handed to Donna, who was more interested in video poker than his offering.

"With all the flak I took from you guys," he said, "now that I have a finished chapter to show, you don't want to look?"

"What would we want that for?" Donna asked dismissively. "Sign a printed copy for me, and we'll talk."

Misty wiped her hands on a towel. She extended her hand to Luke. "Fine," she said. "Gimme."

She ran her finger across the top page. "What the hell is a Daylin?" she asked.

"A character in my book."

"No one names a child Daylin."

"What's the difference between Daylin and, say, Misty?"

"Tons of people are named Misty," Donna said.

"Name one celebrity Misty," Luke demanded.

His friends replied with silence.

Misty held up the stack of paper to Luke. "I'm only trying to help you see that any American will pick up your book and the first thing they'll think is, *What the fuck is a Daylin?*"

"Why don't you change it to something classic?" Donna asked. "Like Shelley, or maybe Priss?"

"Your candidate for a classic name is Priss?"

"My aunt was a Priss," Donna said.

Luke pinched a corner of the stack of paper. "Do you see these watermarks?" he asked. "This is done. Final product."

Donna gave Luke an *I told you so* grin. "You should have checked with Misty first," she said.

The Daylin vs. Priss argument snowballed, and within an hour, the six other diners and drinkers in the place were contributing to a rowdy discussion concerning the strangest names they'd ever encountered. Even Pastor Mangi, out late after baseball practice, chimed in with some unique tags members of his flock had been saddled with over the years.

As Luke got up to leave in a surprisingly sober state, Misty yelled, "I'm going to name my next dog Daylin!"

94

Roger's house was empty. The curios that had once littered the corners of the old man's crusty domicile had been neatly transformed into stacks of cleanly-labeled moving boxes. Two maids bustled about in the kitchen.

"Come grab this tape," he said to Luke, who walked over to Roger in a stupor, dazed by the change in the place. Roger rolled over to a package of hunting magazines, held the box tightly, and Luke sealed it shut.

"Off to the old folks' home, huh?" Luke asked, joking maybe a little.

Roger made a coughing croak. "My ma has a spread in Masonville. She's ninety-eight. She could use some company."

"There's someone on this planet older than you, Roger? I don't believe it."

Roger unlocked his wheelchair and headed outside. Luke followed.

"You're taking off, too, ain't you?" Roger asked.

"Monday."

"Where to?"

"Not sure," Luke said. "New York first."

"I'll give you a helluva deal on this place."

"Why leave?"

"I'm falling apart, kid," he said. "I saw my chest scar in the mirror this morning, and you know what it looked like? A fucked-up upside-down vagina."

"Beautiful," Luke said.

In a slow, proud way, Roger raised a hand to Luke. "Let's finish up," he said dryly.

"Oh, come on," Luke replied, dismissing him. "I'm here for a few more days. What can I do to help?"

"If it's all the same," Roger said, drawing emphasis to his outstretched hand. "Let's check this off the list."

Luke reached into his pocket for a pen. "Let's at least swap addresses," he said.

Roger shook his head. "Not interested."

"What if I want to come for a visit?"

Roger finally pulled his hand back to his lap. "Good luck out there. I hope you make a million bucks."

Their speedy, offhand goodbye ended there, gentlemanly quietude serving as the cap on their brief friendship. As

Roger wheeled into the house, Luke considered rushing up behind the old man, dropping to his knees and embracing him. He'd kiss him on the temple, receive soft pats of shared friendly fervor, then leave him to his lonely chores.

But he didn't.

In the forest on Luke's walk home, the only snow left sat in sleepy shadows.

95

The note was in Luke's mailbox when he returned home from Roger's. Implicitly benign, folded neatly on top of a credit card bill and a Chinese food menu, Luke thought it was a junk flyer until he opened it and learned that the hours he'd wasted in grievous distress about what to do with Anya was all for naught.

He reminded himself it wasn't a break-up. In their months of partnership, they never exchanged any promises, vows, or distinct relationship parameters.

Marion's contribution to the message was a street address in Craiova, Romania. No phone number. Underneath it was words from Anya. In big, curvy letters:

Thank you! XOXO – A.

There Luke stood, his ties to the Romanians officially in hindsight.

Was this heartache he felt? Probably, but it wasn't bad. Truth be told, Luke felt relieved, as though a decision he didn't want to make had been made for him, and now he was off the hook.

The darkest Luke got in the wake of this was when, an hour after he'd read the letter, he had a brain glare of conspiracy that Anya had known how to speak English the whole time.

So many romances are mangled and distorted by failures in communication, and in this narrative, Anya had simply eliminated any potential disorder from the equation. She found a way to get free movies, sex, and warmly mute companionship without having to strike up a conversation or tell any lies.

Luke could drum up any number of fanciful biographies or dossiers for Anya, but none would illuminate anything substantial about her. He didn't know her. He'd seen her naked, trusted the innate physical connection they'd conjured, and she'd disappeared, off to an Eastern Europe Luke couldn't envision.

He woke up the next morning and acknowledged that with his CS discs buried safely in the (*the*, he reminded himself, not *his*) cabin's backyard, he hardly had any luggage whatsoever. The place had come furnished, after all, and while it had brought him great Luddite joy months ago, he had no qualms about leaving the Northern Electric Candlestick for its next renter to dismantle.

All Luke had to bring on the airport shuttle were two bags of non-chipmunk-tainted clothes, three boxes, and whatever he'd clean out of the office later in the day.

Lean and mean.

96

The index cards came off the wall and into the trash, though Luke held onto THAT CAT JUST HAD AN IDEA, figuring it'd make a good gag gift for Lori someday. While some of his notes about the eloquently verbose ways in which he hated William Faulkner gave him a sentimental laugh, these paper ghosts turned out to be inimitably disposable.

He laughed out loud upon finding a stack of them deep in his desk on the subject of his ethereal visitor that had likely been hidden there in a Blotto moment, with his drunk double operating under the clear logic that the paranormal couldn't open drawers.

Had he slain the beast? Hard to say. Whatever it was, it was gone now.

He heard his phone ring. It was Anita, who explained to Luke that galley proofs of the novel were being prepped and that she'd arrange for them to meet in New York to plan the next phase of the process.

He dragged a bag of trash to the yard and embarked on one last walk out past his homestead. Luke ambled among his favorite trees, that infernal grove he loved so much, unsure how he felt about the fact that by this time the next day, he'd be on a big silver bird flying back to the asphalt jungle. This quiet hum of nature would be replaced by jackhammers and ambulance sirens, and Luke felt himself quietly admitting that sounded okay.

He felt confident about his Cornerstone boneyard. With the snow gone, early spring weeds had begun growing over the ragged land, and it looked normal. He considered the trouble these graves might pose further down the line but figured if his ecologically-unsound antics perplexed future cabin inhabitants, any issues would flare long after his security deposit had been returned.

Luke soaked up a view of those woods far off, staring at them intently in an effort to make a deep impression of them in his mind.

Mrs. Packard, watching from across the way, had no idea this marked the last time she'd ever lay eyes on him, this secret murderer and digger, the single most interesting and bizarre neighbor she would ever have.

97

Luke left a fifty dollar tip for Misty after his final dinner at Keene's. She pushed it right back at him. "Buy me a box of wine next time you're in town," she said.

He stood up and put his wallet in his pocket, waiting clumsily for a hug. Misty gave the impression she didn't understand what all the fuss was about. Luke feigned deep offense.

"I spend eight months coming to this joint, and a wave is all I get?"

Misty groaned, threw her towel on her shoulder, and walked *all the way* around the bar to offer a two-second embrace. "Satisfied?" she asked.

She returned to her place behind the bar, politely approaching a fresh-faced woman who sat down in front of a video poker machine.

"What are we drinking?"

The road back to the cabin was less friendly somehow when it wasn't covered in snow. Even without the ripple of wine in his veins, Luke felt loopy, busy saying quiet goodbyes to everything he passed.

In a burst of carburetor chunk, Marion's girlfriend Kristina zoomed past Luke, driving an old truck way above the speed limit. He wondered as the vehicle disappeared up the road if Marion had left that poor Gorgon the same way Anya broke up with him, if that's even what she did.

He pictured Anya's face. He couldn't recall what color her eyes were.

He cleaned the cabin, bringing its elements back to pre-Luke code, and when he found himself wanting to watch TV, he remembered he'd packed it up. Before he powered down the upstairs desktop, preparing it for cardboard hibernation, a chat-program icon graced the screen.

Ray: *We watched your favorite movie with Lori tonight.*
Luke: *And?*

Ray: *She was way into the princess, but bored by the aliens and all that. You need to move in and act as her full-time space tutor to keep her focused on the good stuff.*

Luke: *Finally I can become your number two wife and movie guru to your children.*

Ray: *We were bound to have a gay sci-fi wedding eventually.*

Luke: *You and I should both be so lucky.*

Ray: *GFY.*

Hoping an early bedtime would silence his mind, Luke picked up the sheet and blanket he laid out for himself and flopped on the couch. He did not detect the chipmunk darting across his yard as he switched off the outside light.

98

When Anita shook Luke's hand for the first time, she exhibited a sweetness he would never have predicted based on their thorny phone discussions. She was stylish, elegant, and well-mannered, one of those dashing Southern belles who moonlighted convincingly as a savvy Manhattanite.

He felt strange about the realization, but Luke thought his book editor was *cool.*

Their meeting was heavy with publishing jargon and social media trigger words that genuinely confused Luke. He may have been a Dweeb King once, but his stint in Deer Meadow had transformed him into a bit of a yokel. Dalton, handy at Luke's side, translated the terms discussed, and the conference passed by quickly.

Anita brought out five book cover designs at the end of the hour and arranged for Luke to get an author photo taken. She and Dalton agreed investing in a new suit was priority number one for Mr. Sullivan, seeing as the one he was wearing today (it fit fine a year ago) made him look like a turtle inside an oversized shell.

At lunch, Dalton presented Luke with a gift.

"We loaded it up for you," he said.

Luke rummaged through the bag as the street buzzed behind them. "You'll resist," Dalton said. "But I promise you'll like it."

The tablet was sleek and lighter than Luke expected.

"We put ten e-books on there," Dalton said, which prompted a whine from his friend and client. "Consider it a tool of the new world. Learn it."

A waitress appeared, and Dalton ordered coffees for the two of them.

Returning his focus to Luke, Dalton said, "You did well today."

"Yeah?" Luke asked. "Tell me again how many copies it has to sell to make a profit."

"A lot. More than you think."

Luke stared down the busy boulevard beyond them. "Publication date?"

"This business moves slowly," Dalton said. "It could be a while."

They sat in silence, Dalton recognizing Luke's timid mood. "Just remember," he said. "If you do what your agent and publishers say, you have a 50/50 chance of making a quarter of the money you anticipate earning from this."

Not eliciting a laugh, Dalton slammed his hand on the table. "I have a surprise for you."

99

Luke had returned to the mothership.

It had been at least a year since he'd swapped emails with Kevin Turney at Cornerstone, and when he approached Luke and Dalton in the CS main office lobby in Gramercy, it was though the pope was greeting Luke personally.

Skinny and sharply-dressed, Kevin, sporting a thin beard and short, well-combed hair, was expecting a handshake, but, overtaken in the moment, Luke pulled the poor guy close in an embrace that would have done his pal Marion proud.

Dalton urged Luke to cool it.

Kevin started them off on the tour Dalton had arranged. Within a minute, Luke tuned his companions out completely, experiencing euphoria with every wall poster and newspaper cut-out he passed. This daze ebbed when Kevin introduced Luke to a cadre of Cornerstone employees he once had lengthy online interaction with back at

Dweeb King.

Publicists, researchers, technical consultants – Luke recognized them all by name, inspiring light laughter by introducing himself as Cornerstone's number one stalker, only half-joking.

They wandered through the offices for thirty minutes, and Luke hardly felt like he took a breath the entire time. After Kevin told Luke what new releases they were working on, information typically guarded intensely (Luke promised not to tell, but Gus Van Cant might have some choice forum words later), it was time for the former Dweeb King to leave the building.

He wouldn't go, however, without spending time in The Throne Room. The video clips Cornerstone released at least once a month were the same every time. Somebody like director Marco Cruz (*Ecstasy*, CS#515) or actor Mitch Yeats (*Imminent Injury*, CS#175) would enter the crowded inventory space and have a chance to take home several CS editions from its brimming shelves, as long as each celebrity explained why he chose his favorites.

There was a time Luke claimed it was where he wanted his ashes scattered.

Kevin made it very clear he could only take one DVD – Luke was no Marco Cruz – and as he and Dalton kicked into a conversation about the Yankees' disastrous season, Luke walked into the closet-sized room alone.

It was industrial and plain, metal shelves hiding blandly-painted walls. Luke couldn't help but notice Cornerstone Standard organized their releases by name and not by spine number, which to his OCD collector's instincts was beautifully bizarre.

He investigated old LaserDiscs piled on the floor, felt the heft of some of the studio's elaborate box sets, and traced his finger along the CS logos on their smooth spines.

Luke allowed himself five minutes in the room, not exactly on the verge of tears, but thinking he might get there.

This was it. It was all here. Well, the past was here.

Luke Sullivan shed his Dweeb King skin in that Throne Room, hiding it behind the films on the shelves, in their shadows.

When he emerged empty-handed, Kevin reminded him that even if he had eyes for one of their more expensive out-of-print titles, he could make that happen.

"That's okay," Luke said. "I have everything I need."

100

I hate the women in these magazines, but I always flip through them. Waiting for my white chocolate mocha, me and my celebrities. I love her top. I need to go shopping, pick up something for brunch on Sunday, but I want to stay in the air conditioning. It's so hot already. Is it really only May? I like this bookstore more than the one near the house. I don't run into anybody, and nobody can catch me ordering extra whipped cream on my drink, which is being handed to me right now, thank you, put the magazine back. I should buy one of those presidential biographies for the girls to give daddy for Father's Day, but has he read them all? He's been flying so much. I don't want to pick up her new one. Even in paperback that mystery she put out last year was almost a thousand pages. It took me the whole summer. I didn't even finish it. Start it again? All the way from the beginning? No, thanks. This new one is 30% off, though. Maybe I'll convince the girls to make it one for book club. I love that lowest part of the whipped cream just above the drink. I wish I could save it for last. Okay. New Arrivals. It's not here. Now, wait. Where did I hear about this other one? Radio interview, it must have been. The lettering on this back cover is so small. That guy! He looks different than he did on TV. Dedication page. *To Roger.* No table of contents. Numbered chapters. The first line. *I'm not sure when he died, but I killed him on Thursday.* Pretty good hook. 253 pages, not too bad. Oh, but where's the 30% off sticker? When it goes on sale, or I'll wait for the paperback. One of these days.

This book was written in Incline Village, NV
and Seattle, WA.

The author would like to thank his literary Tahoe allies:
Liz Blaustein, Peggy Bourland, Brian and Maggie Browder,
Arturo Coloma, Jackie and Steve Dontcho, Candy Elwood,
Jeff Gulden, Lori Hébert, Kelly Heslin, Thaddeus Homan,
Mike Miller, Marc Roberts, Bob and Connie Skidmore,
Jan and Mike Turney, Roger Ulrich, Daylin Wade,
Muggsy Walnut, and John and Paulette Young.

And to the family who witnessed and tolerated the author's
delirium firsthand: Mic and Maddy, Christina and Joe, Sarah,
Brian and Sara, Odin and Graham, Chris and Karin,
Kathy and Tom, Josh and Tomiré, Mary Ann,
Ily and Clavey, Cindy, and Krym'z.

The Modern Library 100
www.themodernlibrary.com